"We haven't finished, Jenny. You owe me."

Mark's words brought an indignant flush to Jenny's cheeks.

"I owe you nothing!" she snapped furiously, feeling her heart start to pound. She had to get hold of herself or she was lost. She hadn't been a match for him before, and nothing had changed since. It couldn't be love she felt for him, so it must be a kind of fear. She should have got out while the going was good.

"Don't panic," Mark said smoothly, taking full note of her wide eyes that so clearly mirrored her thoughts. "We've plenty of time. I don't intend to rush you. This time you'll come to me...."

OTHER
Harlequin Romances
by JANE CORRIE

Many of these titles are available at your local bookseller
or through the Harlequin Reader Service.

For a free catalogue listing all available Harlequin Romances,
send your name and address to:

HARLEQUIN READER SERVICE
M.P.O. Box 707, Niagara Falls, N.Y. 14302
Canadian address: Stratford, Ontario, Canada N5A 6W2

or use coupon at back of book.

Peacock's Walk

by

JANE CORRIE

Harlequin Books

TORONTO • LONDON • NEW YORK • AMSTERDAM
SYDNEY • HAMBURG • PARIS

Original hardcover edition published in 1978
by Mills & Boon Limited

ISBN 0-373-02209-3

Harlequin edition published November 1978

Printed in Canada

CHAPTER ONE

JENNY GRANGE studied the menu that had just been handed in for her approval, and tried to give the listed fare her full attention, but after a second or so, she gave it up and thrust the printed sheet away from her with an impatient movement. Tony could be trusted to do all that was necessary, and there was no need for her to approve or disapprove of his selection for the evening meal.

Her wide grey-green eyes softened as she thought of Tony, who must now be in his seventies, and had worked at Peacock's Walk since his early twenties, starting at the scullery level and working his way up to head chef—a position he had held for as long as Jenny could remember.

A small sigh escaped her as her eye caught the register book on the other side of her desk, and she pulled it towards her and opened it. There were several signatures that had been added since she had last seen it, but the one she sought stood out in bold strokes, like the man himself, she thought, as her gaze lingered on it. Mark Chanter hadn't changed a bit, if his signature was anything to go by, and that meant he hadn't forgotten, or forgiven her, for what he had considered as an act of betrayal on her part.

Her musings were curtailed by a brusque knock on the door and Tony entered. His chef's hat was slightly askew, and gave Jenny a hint of his mood. He pointed to the open register on her desk and looked back at her. 'So you've seen it, have you? That fool of a girl should have said we were booked up,' he growled.

Giving him what she hoped was an admonishing look, yet knowing full well it would have no effect whatsoever, Jenny replied mildly, 'It's a free country, Tony—and that fool of a girl, as you call her, has only been with us a year or so. The name wouldn't mean a thing to her, now would it?'

At this point the aforesaid maligned girl stalked into the office, and Jenny, seeing the look of outraged dignity on her face felt a pang of exasperation; she had obviously heard the comments passed. 'You keep to your side of the business,' Rose Smith interjected swiftly to Tony, and turned to Jenny with an apologetic look in her brown eyes. 'I'm sorry, Miss Grange, honestly I am. How could I have known he was *the* Mark Chanter?' she pleaded.

Jenny gave her a smile. 'I'm not blaming you, Rose,' she said soothingly, and looking back to where Tony stood with a scowl on his face, added, 'As I've told Mr Bart, this is a hotel—not a private residence. Mr Chanter is a guest, and will be treated as one.'

Rose gave a sniff of appreciation at this, and gave

Tony a look of triumph before taking her leave with a gratified, 'Thank you, Miss Grange.'

Jenny watched her departing figure and felt very depressed. So much for her thinking Mark's name wouldn't mean anything to her! She would now set about finding out the reason why such a personage as Mark Chanter should want to stay at a little-known hotel on the outskirts of Brighton, when he owned a string of luxury hotels—one of which lay in the centre of Brighton itself. If Tony had not made such a fuss, the visit would not have caused much speculation, she thought miserably, but now the whole place would be buzzing with the news.

Her eyes met Tony's brooding ones, and she shook her head at him in a weary gesture. 'Oh, Tony!' she said with a hint of impatience in her voice. 'If I can forget, why can't you? It's two years now, and although I confess I'm puzzled as to why he should honour us with his presence, I see no reason to rake up the past.' Her gaze went back to the door through which Rose had just passed. 'If you hadn't made such a fuss the visit could have passed without comment,' she shrugged, 'or at least been put down to an odd whim on his part, but there's little likelihood of that now. Rose had her Sherlock Holmes look on her face when she left, and you know what that means,' she added significantly.

Tony pushed his cap yet further back on his head and gave a shrug. 'Think he's found out we're on the rocks?' he queried, not bothering to give Rose another thought.

Jenny frowned at him. 'It's not that bad!' she

answered, trying to force a note of firmness in her voice, but she couldn't fool Tony.

'Remember me?' he asked, his normally dour expression breaking into one of his rare smiles. 'You can't pull the wool over my eyes.' His frown returned as his glance rested on the visitors' book. 'I'd say someone tipped him the wink,' he said darkly. 'Can't trust the staff nowadays, haven't a notion of what loyalty means.'

Jenny said nothing, he was very probably right, she thought, there wasn't much he missed. He was probably right about the reason Mark was there too. 'What if he wants to buy me out, will you stay?' she queried softly.

His answer was definite. 'Not if he wants you out!' he answered grimly.

Jenny pushed back a strand of golden hair that had clung to her cheek. She had thought that would be his attitude, and knew better than to try and change his mind. She smiled at him, although the smile did not reach her eyes. 'We could always start a restaurant somewhere,' she suggested with a quirk of her soft lips. 'Right next to one of his hotels.'

Tony gave her a searching look. 'Sure; about time someone stood up to big business crowding out the small fry,' he growled.

Jenny sighed and closed the register with a snap. 'I do feel I've let you all down,' she said miserably. 'I'm sure if I'd had more business acumen I would have made a success of it.'

'Now don't go blaming yourself,' admonished Tony gently. 'We were doing fine until the opposi-

tion moved in. There was no one to touch us for
service or cuisine, but we couldn't compete with
Chanter's up-to-date four star efforts—so you can
stop whipping yourself on that count.' He nodded
gently to himself. 'Been wondering how long he'd
wait before making his move,' he said ruminatively.

Jenny gave him a look of resigned patience. 'You
never see things from a business point of view,
Tony,' she said sadly. 'Can't you understand why
he would be interested? We're in just the right
position for an organisation such as his. If it were
anyone else, you wouldn't have queried their
motives, now would you?' she demanded.

Tony gave her a stern look under grey beetling
brows. 'But it's not anyone else, is it?' he replied
dourly. 'The trouble with you, Goldilocks, is that
you can never see the wood for the trees, and you're
in it before you know it.'

Jenny looked away hastily at the familiar use of a
nickname Tony had given her since she was a
toddler, and it was no use pretending she didn't
know what he was talking about. Her full lips
firmed as she looked back at him. 'Do you really
think I'd be fool enough to get hurt a second time?'
she asked sardonically.

With a touch of ruefulness in his eyes, Tony
leaned over towards her and patted her on the hand.
'That's what I'm trying to prevent,' he said gently.
'I just wanted to make sure, that's all—I wouldn't
have brought it up otherwise. Don't go getting soft
over him again. He walked all over you last time,
then threw you over on the flimsiest excuse,' he held

a commanding hand up to stop the words of protest Jenny was about to utter. 'Like I said before,' he went on firmly, 'Jealous or not, no man worth his salt ends an engagement on the say-so of a friend— not when that friend has set his sights on the same girl. Anyone with half an eye could see how it was with Malcolm Peacock, and Mark Chanter's no fool, he'd have had to be blind not to spot that Malcolm wanted you.'

His eyes softened as they rested on Jenny's bowed head. 'I'm not enjoying bringing this up, Goldie, but I promised your dad I'd look out for you.' He gave a loud sigh. 'The trouble is, you're too soft, a pushover for a man like Chanter. Just remember what happened before, that's all I'm asking. I told you when it happened, and I'll tell you again, I think he wanted out of the engagement, and grabbed at the chance offered. He's not the marrying type, sweetie, so watch your step.'

Jenny sat for a long time at her desk after Tony had left her. She very much resented the 'too soft' tag he had so dogmatically labelled her with. It might have been true two years ago, but not now. She had had to learn a few hard facts since then, but she was not bitter, a little wiser perhaps, and able to understand Tony's forthright comments, and although she knew his fears were groundless, she was a little surprised that he still saw her as a child in need of protection.

From what? she thought sadly. From his own admission, he didn't think Mark had really cared for her, and after many days of heartache she had been

forced to come to the same conclusion. His whirl-
wind courtship of her had left her breathless. He
had been extremely demanding and very possessive,
and if Jenny's father had not died soon after going
down with pleurisy, they would now be married. As
it was, a decent interval had had to elapse before the
date could be fixed.

Her lovely eyes lingered on the brown velvet curtaining of her office window as she went back to that
time. A time when she did not own Peacock's Walk,
but had been secretary to the owner, Michael Peacock. Her father had been manager of the hotel,
then, and had occupied a small suite on the ground
floor, and Jenny had been brought up to regard the
hotel as her home, as indeed it was, and since she
had been motherless from the age of five, the hotel
staff had rallied round to take turns in watching
over her. There had never been a time when
Jenny had no one to turn to, she could lay claim
to at least four 'mothers' and any number of sympathetic 'uncles'. She could have been exceedingly
spoilt, but such was her nature that she never took
anything for granted, and never failed to show her
appreciation for the little pleasures thought up for
her enjoyment.

Her eyes left the curtains and centred on the large
oak chair the other side of the room. That had been
Malcolm's chair, and she closed her eyes for a
moment or so while the memories washed over her.
Malcolm had been ten years older than her, and the
only son of the proprietor, and like Jenny, had also
been brought up at Peacock's Walk. Although most

of his life had been spent at an exclusive boarding school, he did come home for holidays, and despite the age gap, he and Jenny had been very close. To Jenny, he was the big brother she had never had, and it wasn't until his death in a car crash two years ago that she found out just what she was to him.

None of this had she been able to convey to a furious Mark, who had accused her of duplicity when she and Malcolm had missed the last train back after a business trip up North, and had been forced to put up at an hotel in Aberdeen for one night.

There had been so much that Jenny had not been able to understand at that time, but pieces of the puzzle had gradually filled in during the months that followed the ending of her engagement to Mark.

The letter that Malcom had left her, for one thing, had shown her a very different aspect of the past, and one that had never before occurred to her. She did know that Malcolm was against her engagement to Mark, and did all in his power to break off their association. It was through Malcolm that Jenny had met Mark, for the two men were, or had been, close friends, for Mark had attended the same university as Malcolm, and it was natural that they should become friends. They had the same interests and the same backgrounds, and would eventually take over the running of their respective parents' businesses.

When Malcolm had returned from a business trip abroad to find Mark firmly ensconced as Jenny's constant companion, he had been furious at what he had called Mark's 'undercover activities' and set about educating Jenny on the facts of life. A slightly amused Jenny had listened to him, demurring only when he had said that Mark would eventually hurt her badly. He had known Chanter for a very long time, he had told her; he used women as playthings, and was never serious. He went on to tell her that he did not intend to stand by and watch her get hurt as other women had been hurt.

At this point Jenny moved restlessly, and tried to turn her thoughts to other matters, but they persisted. If only she had known then that Malcolm loved her, and that it had been sheer jealousy that had made him act as he had. She recalled her feelings when she read the letter he had left for her, the letter that had been given to Tony for safe keeping, to be given to her if anything happened to him.

'—if you ever read this letter I shall have met with some unforeseen fate. There is so much I want to tell you, my darling. So much you never saw—such as how much I loved you. There was never anyone else but you, for me. That you are reading this letter means that I have lost you—perhaps Mark does deserve you, but I do not regret acting as I did, and if given the same opportunity I would not hesitate to do all in my power to wrest you from him. I always looked upon you as mine, and the thought of someone else possessing you was not to be borne. I would rather it this way than to stand by and see you marry another.

'Forgive me, my darling, for the lies I told Chanter about our association, hoping to make him throw you over, but I didn't succeed, did I? I can only wish you happiness, my love, and remember I did what I did because I loved you.'

Jenny's gaze went to Malcolm's chair again, and she said softly, 'But you did succeed, Malcolm. Your will saw to that.' Her eyes went to her hands. She couldn't blame Malcolm for wanting to provide for her if he wasn't there to watch over her, but it was the straw that broke the camel's back where Mark was concerned. His furious reaction and his harsh words still remained etched in her mind. 'So much for your "good friends" act,' he had sneered when it was learnt that Malcolm had left her Peacock's Walk. 'It's the done thing to provide for your mistress, isn't it?' he had taunted her savagely. 'Well, I hope it was worth it, because we're through!'

That had been two years ago, and the last time she had seen Mark. She had tried to send him his ring back, but he had returned it with a terse message that she was to keep it as a memento of the good times they had had. This had hurt Jenny much more than any of his previous accusations, and he must have known it would, for he was telling her that if she had hoped her action in returning the ring would bring him back to her, then it had failed.

A bewildered Jenny had had no such thought in mind. The sudden turn of events had left her completely numb. To be so sought after, and courted at

the speed of a cyclone, for such had been Mark's
courtship of her, only to find herself thrown aside
as a shop-soiled article, had left her badly shaken.

Recalling Tony's worry that she was still vulner-
able to Mark, Jenny gave a small bitter smile. Tony
knew of the letter Malcom had left her, but did
not know of its contents, and that had Jenny wished
to get Mark back she only need show him that letter.
But she hadn't, and when she had recovered from
the blow of Malcolm's death, followed so closely
by Mark's abrupt removal from the scene, she had
wondered why, and had eventually come to the conclusion that she had not been as much in love with
Mark as she had thought she was.

There had been plenty of time since then to mull
over the past, and one fact had stood out starkly.
Mark had given her no choice but to accept his
courtship. He was a very determined man, and she
was now of the opinion that it had been like being
in the middle of a cyclone—you couldn't withstand
it, but had to go along with it. She could see how
it had happened, for Mark was not only good-
looking, but possessed a dynamic personality, one
that swept you along with him, whether you wanted
to go or not. He was also very experienced, and
Jenny had been no match for him—not that she
had viewed his interest in her as such at the time.
She had to admit to feeling extremely flattered that
such a man should set his sights on her and want to
marry her, and if it hadn't been for Malcolm, he
would have married her.

Jenny got up quickly and walked over to the window in an effort to shake these thoughts off. If Mark was in the hotel, then he was there for a purpose, and Tony's suspicions that he had come to make an offer for the hotel would be a certainty, for Jenny could see no other reason for the visit. Going over the past was not going to help her to remain subjective and see things from a business point of view—the very thing she had accused Tony of not so long ago, she told herself crossly—although she had more reason than he had for adopting this attitude. It wasn't easy to forget that Mark had accused her of being Malcolm's mistress, even though events had since proved to her that Malcolm must have hinted at such an association, for he was as determined to end their engagement as Mark had been to bring it about.

The ringing of the telephone on her desk cut short these memories from the past, and the dulcet tones of Rose came over the wire asking if Miss Grange could see Mr Chanter.

Taking a deep breath, Jenny thought that he hadn't wasted much time; he hadn't altered in that respect either. 'Very well,' she answered smoothly, adding quickly, 'Oh, Rose, would you please hold back coffee until I ring for it?' she requested, afraid that her visitor might feel that she was presuming on their past acquaintance if she offered him refreshment.

A few seconds later there was a perfunctory knock on her office door, and Mark strode in.

Jenny did not move from her position, but gave him a small smile purely for the sake of politeness, which was not returned, she noticed, and as he walked towards her she watched him curiously, telling herself that this was the man she very nearly married, but found the fact hard to accept. He was still extremely good-looking; dark and lithe of movement. His blue-grey eyes that had once laughed into hers were now devoid of emotion, and as his glance flickered over her she wondered if he was thinking the same as she was. If so, there was no outward sign of such thoughts on his hard features. With a kind of surprised relief Jenny acknowledged that they were now strangers, and that being the case, the discussion she presumed they were about to have should present no difficulty to either of them.

After seating himself in Malcolm's chair, he came straight to the point with an abrupt, 'It's rumoured that you're in financial difficulties. Is that correct?' he demanded without preamble.

Jenny stiffened at the bald question; he had made it sound more like an accusation than a question. His autocratic acquisition of Malcolm's chair had not helped her to retain her cool approach to the situation. He knew very well that it was Malcolm's chair, and could have chosen another, the one in front of her desk, for instance, but that would have looked as if she was interviewing him, and on no account would he allow such a state of affairs to exist, she thought scathingly. It also occurred to her that Tony had been right again in assuming that someone on the staff must have given him this information. Lifting her chin a fraction higher, she replied haughtily, 'It's not quite as bad as that, Mr Chanter.'

Her use of his surname seemed to infuriate him, and his eyes blazed back into hers before he answered furiously, 'Don't come the grand lady with me, Jenny Grange. I've a long memory where you're concerned. You're damn lucky to be sitting where you are, and don't forget that. Not every secretary ends up owning the establishment she worked for!'

Jenny flushed and looked away from him and down at the desk in front of her. So much for her thinking it was going to be easy! They were back to the past with a vengeance, and he was once again speaking to her as if she were a cheap go-getter. For a second or so she debated whether to ring the bell for Thomas, the hall porter, and have him escort him out of the hotel, not that she could envisage such a happening actually taking place, but the thought gave her a pleasant feeling. It was too ridiculous for words, she told herself, and made an attempt to bring the conversation to a less personal nature. 'I'm sure you had a reason for asking to see me,' she managed to say calmly. 'I think the past's best left out of it, don't you?' she added briskly.

He gave a curt nod to this gentle but firm reply to his deliberately goading remarks. 'And I'm sure you're aware of the reason. I wish to purchase Peacock's Walk,' he said harshly. 'Name your price; I won't quibble over it.'

Jenny gave a small bitter smile at this. He could afford not to 'quibble' as he had put it. She looked up from the desk and met his gaze squarely before she replied slowly, 'If I sell, it will only be under certain conditions.' She saw him start and stare at her, and wondered what he was thinking. That she would demand to stay, perhaps? This was her home when all was said and done, but she had no such thought in mind. 'The staff would have to be kept on,' she went on firmly, adding quickly, 'I intend to make my own arrangements, of course.'

She did not miss his quick speculative look at her as she said this, and she waited for his answer, thinking that she might be able to persuade Tony to stay on. He could hold a watching brief over the interests of the staff under the new regime.

Mark Chanter's eyes left hers and centred on the register on the desk, and the look said more than words to Jenny. It plainly said that he didn't think the staff quite measured up to his standards. To his way of thinking, the fall-off of guests bore mute witness to this.

Jenny could see his point, but felt it was unfair criticism. It was not the staff's fault that past patrons of Peacock's Walk had been enticed away by the plushier Chanter Enterprise, or that the money Malcolm had hoped would be forthcoming for the slight modernisations he had in mind would not be available. The sudden collapse of the travel agency he had started in Rome, a few months before his death, had taken all available funds, and there were still debts owing. Debts that had to be paid out of the hotel's profits, such as they were.

'I'm afraid I can't agree to that,' he replied haughtily. 'There may be a few I would wish to retain,' he conceded grudgingly. 'But to take them en bloc is out of the question.'

Jenny's lips firmed at this; he would take the younger staff was what he meant. The older ones had been with the hotel for most of their working lives, and were hardly likely to find other positions, and it was for this reason that she had made the stipulation. Not that these sentiments would mean anything to Mark Chanter, she thought bitterly. Sentimentality didn't enter into his world—as if he hadn't enough money. It wouldn't hurt him to keep the older staff on. They might not work at break-neck speed, but at least you could be sure that whatever work they were given would be carried out with meticulous care. She thought of Tony. 'Tony?' she asked quietly.

He gave her a long speculative look. Tony was more than an employee to her, and Mark knew it. He shrugged offhandedly. 'He must be due for retirement,' he said dryly, but it told Jenny all she wanted to know. His answer had given her her answer.

She looked down at her hands and was a little surprised to find them tightly clenched together. 'I'm sorry,' she replied in a low voice, 'I'm afraid there's no point in our going on with this discussion. I said all the staff, and I meant it.' She stood up quickly to indicate that the interview was over.

He took his time in standing up, and his hard jaw showed his fury at being dismissed so perfunctorily. 'Because of Tony?' he grated out harshly. 'No wonder the place is dying on its feet! You might have been a good secretary, but you've no idea how to run an hotel. Business and sentiment do not mix, Miss Grange.' He walked to the door and paused before he opened it. 'You'll find it hard to get a buyer on those stipulations,' he added furiously, 'and don't,' he flung back at her before he left, 'take too long in changing your mind, will you? or I might just leave you to stew in the financial mess you've made of things!'

It took a few minutes for Jenny to pull herself together after Mark had left, and the arrival of the coffee tray came as a much needed stimulant. To her annoyance, she found she was actually trembling, and had to make a firm effort to control her hand as she poured herself a cup of steaming hot liquid. How could she have ever thought she was in love with such a man? she asked herself incredulously, and decided that she had had an extremely narrow escape when he had thrown her over. It would have been like being married to a computer. Statistics were all he was interested in. Little things like understanding and trust simply did not exist in his world. No, he hadn't changed one bit; he was still the same man who hadn't even bothered to give her a hearing when she had tried to explain her relationship with Malcolm.

As for changing her mind—Jenny's cup joined the saucer with a dull clink—she wouldn't dream of it! She would sell Peacock's Walk—she hadn't any option now. Mark Chanter must have been pretty sure of his ground to have added that loaded rider about the financial state of the hotel. He had probably heard of the collapse of the travel agency from the same source that had given him the rest of his information, but that didn't matter now. One thing she did know, and that was that Chanter Enterprises would not own Peacock's Walk, come what may. She would even be prepared to sell at a loss rather than see it go to Mark Chanter!

CHAPTER TWO

By the time Jenny had finished her coffee, Tony had joined her, and as she had been expecting him, she took an extra cup out of her filing cabinet, one that she kept for such occasions, and poured him some coffee.

'He made an offer?' asked Tony seating himself on the corner of her desk and accepting the cup she held out to him.

Jenny nodded, and concentrated on squeezing the remains of the coffee pot into her cup.

'And he wants you out?' persisted Tony, determined to hear all of it.

'All of the staff—or rather the older ones,' she corrected slowly. 'I said no,' she looked up at the frowning Tony. 'It doesn't matter about me, but I do owe the staff something after all these years with the firm. I simply refuse to sell unless they are kept on.'

She was silent for a short while, then said suddenly, 'We'll advertise, Tony. You were right—we can't keep going much longer without capital.' She gave a sigh. 'It might have been possible if the travel agency hadn't collapsed. I'm still waiting to hear from the solicitor about the final settlement.'

Tony nodded gloomily. 'Any idea of how much you still owe?' he asked sympathetically.

Jenny gave a light shrug of her slim shoulders as she answered dryly, 'All I know is that if it's over five thousand, then I shall have to sell to clear it.'

Putting his cup down heavily on the desk, Tony replied briskly, 'Right, so we advertise. No point in prolonging the agony.' He rubbed his chin thoughtfully. 'You know, it might be a bit of a job getting someone to take it under those conditions.'

Jenny's eyes left his and she concentrated on the coffee jug. 'So Mark Chanter just told me,' she said quietly. 'But it won't stop me trying.' She went on in a firmer voice, 'You never know, we might be lucky and get some tycoon who doesn't have a clue about hotel management, but fancies owning one. And it's not as if we were stuck in some high street,' she added on a brighter note. 'We've an acre of grounds, remember, and that makes the place quite exclusive.'

'Which is why Chanter wanted it?' said Tony, darting a quick speculative look at Jenny.

She frowned at him but refused to rise to the bait and discuss old scores. 'It might have been,' she conceded. 'Either way, it doesn't matter now. He's out of it.' The last words were said with a great deal of emphasis and Tony's brows raised, but he wisely did not comment.

When Tony left her a short while later, Jenny set about wording out the advertisement that was to go in all the leading monthly journals that catered for such transactions, not forgetting their American counterparts, because she was convinced that she would be successful in acquiring the right buyer. It wasn't, she told herself brightly, as if the older staff were in their dotage, although Mark Chanter had hinted as much. They were all in their late fifties, it was true, apart from Tony that was, and still had a few years of good service left.

A little later, Jenny stared at the carefully worded advertisement that stated that a select hotel standing in one acre of wooded grounds was up for sale, and experienced a feeling of utter desolation. Seeing the cold impersonal words brought home the full implication of what she was doing. She had never imagined such a happening coming to pass, and had tried to hold off the inevitable for months now, hoping against hope that something might be salvaged out of the wreckage, and it might have done, if Malcolm hadn't had a whim to start that agency. He wasn't to know, of course, that it would fail. He hadn't known that Mark Chanter would invade their territory either, giving the already crippled hotel a final blow that was impossible to recover from.

Shaking these thoughts away, she tried to regain her earlier optimistic outlook, but was soon cast down into the depths again at the thought of her next step. She must inform the staff of her decision to sell. It wouldn't do for them to find out about it in a roundabout manner. At the thought of Rose, she sighed heavily; no doubt she was busy putting two and two together, and would soon be dropping a few heavy hints to whoever cared to listen to her.

Taking a deep breath, she rang reception and asked Rose to contact Mrs Hooney, and ask her to call and see her when she had a few minutes to spare,

Mrs Hooney, a stout motherly woman, who had worked at Peacock's Walk almost as long as Tony had, walked into Jenny's office a short while later, and pulling down her starched cuffs over her uniform sleeves, she smiled at Jenny. 'You wanted to see me, hinny?'

Jenny swallowed at her use of an old endearment. Dodie Hooney wasn't an employee either, not in the strict sense of the word, for she had been one of the few who had 'mothered' her, all those years ago.

'Sit down, Dodie,' Jenny said gently. 'I've some news for you that won't be very welcome, I'm afraid.' She swallowed again; might as well get it over with, she thought miserably. 'I'm having to sell the hotel,' she got out quickly as her worried eyes met the brown ones of the older woman.

Dorothy Hooney, or Dodie, as Jenny had called her since her babyhood, not being able to pronounce her name properly, gave Jenny a reassuring smile. 'Reckon you hadn't much choice, lass,' she said quietly, leaning forward towards her as if to offer comfort. 'Don't worry about us older ones. We'll be retiring soon anyway, and I'm sure most of us have a bit put away. It's you we're worried about.' She sniffed. 'I overheard that Rose talking to Thomas this morning. Seems she's got it all worked out. Said Mark Chanter was taking over,' she gave Jenny a searching look. 'I said he'd be the last person you'd sell to.' She hesitated a second or so, and Jenny knew she was not stating an opinion but asking a question, and was devoutly grateful that she could support her supposition, and gave a small nod that received a satisfied look from Dodie, who went on in a brisker fashion to say,

'Told them so, but they wouldn't listen. Not the young ones anyway. Us older-staff know how it was,' she added darkly, then gave a wry grin. 'Happen they've a disappointment coming. You should have seen the way that new chambermaid and the girl we took on to give Len a help in the bar smartened themselves up after Rose had told them who was taking over—or who she thought was taking over,' she amended with quiet satisfaction.

She looked back at Jenny. 'What will you do, love?' she asked, then shook her head sadly. 'Young Malcolm was a good lad, but he hadn't his father's business sense. Happen you wouldn't be in this mess, else,' she added dolefully.

Jenny's eyes softened as they rested momentarily on the brown hair tinged with grey. Trust Dodie to understand how it was, never for one moment putting it down to Jenny's mismanagement, as Mark Chanter had, and no doubt a few of the younger staff. 'I can always go back to secretarial work, Dodie,' she replied with a smile. 'I can't say I was cut out to run a business. Besides, it will be nice not to be in the front line for a change, and let someone else do the worrying.'

Dodie eyed her thoughtfully, and nodded sagely.

'Aye, you've had your share of that, true enough. But you take a holiday first—I don't recall you taking one since you took over,' she advised Jenny sternly.

Having got that business out of the way, Jenny left it to Dodie to tell the rest of the staff of her decision to sell, for although Jenny ran the managerial side of things, Dodie had continued to manage the hotel staff, as she had done before Jenny had inherited the hotel.

Recalling what Dodie had said about Mark Chanter being the last person she would sell to, Jenny gave a small sigh of exasperation. Tony, it seemed, was not the only one who was of the opinion that she was still carrying a torch for Mark, and hadn't forgiven him for throwing her over. She hated to think what Dodie would have said if Mark had agreed to her terms and taken over the hotel. Very probably given her a lecture much on the same lines as Tony had, she thought wryly, and was relieved that Mark had not agreed to her terms, it had saved her a lot of explaining in the long run.

Having set things in motion, there was nothing more for Jenny to do but to sit back and await what she hoped would be an answer to her problems. She tried not to think ahead of what she would do after the hotel had been sold. Time enough for that when it happened, she told herself stoutly.

If she had had any qualms or second thoughts about taking such a step, these were soon dispelled by a letter from her solicitor advising her of the final settlement required in the dragged-out saga of the travel agency. It was as she had feared, and as she had gloomily predicted to Tony, almost five thousand pounds. She had no choice now but to sell, and the appended message that advised her that she would be given reasonable time to settle the account came as cold comfort, but she was grateful all the same.

The reply Jenny had hoped to receive, came a fortnight later. There had been several interested replies to the advertisement, but none fitted the 'tycoon' range she had set her heart on, and as she read the letter postmarked 'New York', her spirits rose higher than they had been for months.

Silas P. Hawter was, he informed her, a retired banker, and had been toying with the idea of buying such a property in England. His agent was at that moment in London, and would be getting in touch with Miss Grange directly. He went on to say that he had complete confidence in his agent's judgment and had given him the authority to close the deal should the premises be suitable for his requirements. He ended by saying that in the event of it being a successful transaction, he hoped to make a personal visit in due course of time.

Jenny's hand shook as she laid the letter down. Silas P. Hawter was tailor-made! just what she had hoped for, because what would a retired banker know of hotel management? She blinked as she touched the letter again, and felt like pinching herself to make certain she was not dreaming. Her eyes shone as she went over the possibilities such a transaction might bring in it's wake. There was a

tremendous possibility that the present staff would
be kept on—perhaps she could stay, too?—she shook
her head slowly. It would be enough if the staff
could stay, she couldn't ask for more.

When she showed the letter to Tony later that
day, she was exasperated by his lack of enthusiasm.
'He doesn't mention keeping it on as a hotel, does
he?' he remarked gloomily. 'He might have other
ideas, such as making it his private residence, so
don't go getting excited about it,' he cautioned her.

Jenny gave him an impatient look, but after meeting his earnest brown eyes, gave a small smile.
'Well,' she conceded slowly, 'I suppose he might
have something like that in mind, but he doesn't
say that either, does he?' she appealed to him hopefully.

'Or,' added Tony darkly, 'He may want to turn
the place into an exclusive gambling den. He might
be working for a syndicate.'

Jenny's eyes widened at this and she stared at
Tony. He wouldn't do that, surely? Her soft lips
clamped together firmly. 'Then I shall refuse to
sell,' she replied steadily. 'No matter how much he
offers.' She gave Tony an accusing look. 'Now you've
spoilt everything!' she complained. 'And I was so
sure he was the answer to our problems.'

Tony's sour countenance broke into a grin.
'Someone's got to think of these things, Goldie,' he
said unrepentantly. 'That way you won't be too disappointed if things don't work out. I'm not saying
you're wrong, but don't go throwing your hat over
the windmill yet. We'll wait and see what this agent

of his has to say first,' he advised gently.

In spite of Tony's doleful advice on caution, Jenny soon found herself back in the land of high hopes. Tony meant well, and was only trying to save her from sharp disappointment should his gloomy predictions prove correct, but she had this unshakable feeling that luck was on her side, and that her hopes would be realised.

For the next day or so, she was on tenterhooks waiting for a communication from Silas P. Hawter's agent, and knew a vast sense of relief when the greatly anticipated letter arrived from a Mr Moore, stating that acting as Mr Hawter's agent, he wished to make an appointment to view the premises at the earliest opportunity. Jenny lost no time in answering the letter, suggesting two dates in the near future for the visit, one of which was in three days from the time of writing, and was the date accepted by Mr Moore, who rang to confirm the appointment upon receipt of the letter.

It would not have surprised Jenny if Tony had insisted on being present at the interview, since this would have been his way of protecting her interests, but he contented himself with a, 'Don't sign anything,' comment, and left her to it, although she was sure he would give the agent a pretty thorough visual inspection, on his arrival at the hotel—from a concealed position, that was, and she also knew that if he didn't like what he saw, then he would attend the interview, whether she liked it or not.

As soon as Jenny saw Mr Moore, she felt a surge

of relief flow over her. She hadn't quite known what she was expecting him to look like, but Tony's gloomy forecasts had prompted a certain amount of trepidation, and she had wondered how she would cope if he turned out to be one of the pushy types of agent, out to satisfy the needs of his client come what may.

Now, as she shook hands with the pleasant middle-aged man, she knew her fears had been groundless, and looked forward to their coming conference.

Two hours later a flushed and excited Jenny dared Tony to try and dampen her elation, for the discussion had far exceeded her wildest hopes, as she explained to him, 'He does want to keep the place going as a hotel. He actually requested that the staff be kept on, and . . .' she added with sparkling eyes, 'that includes me. Of course,' she tacked on thoughtfully, 'I wouldn't have the final say on big decisions, sort of manager's position, I suppose you'd call it.' She smiled at Tony happily. 'As if I'd mind that! No more worrying, is how I'd put it, and what a relief that's going to be!' she sighed contentedly.

Tony surveyed her gleaming eyes and flushed countenance. 'Seems to be a little too pat for my liking,' he said cautiously. 'Almost,' he mused, 'as if he knew our circumstances.'

Jenny's smile faded and she gave an exaggerated sigh. 'Must you always look for catches?' she said crossly. 'As for knowing our circumstances, as a matter of fact, he does,' she added, giving a quick grin at the look of surprise on Tony's face. 'It appears that a friend of his knew Malcolm, and this friend used to spend a few days here when he was attending a conference. Well,' she went on, her voice showing her satisfaction, 'this friend saw the advertisement, and knowing that Silas Hawter was in the market for just such a property, told him about it. Mr Moore told me Silas Hawter had explained it all to him when he gave him the authority to close the deal if everything was satisfactory.'

Jenny put her head on one side and surveyed the still unconvinced Tony. 'There's something else I haven't told you,' she said triumphantly. 'We've not only got a buyer, we've got a ready made market, too! This friend of Mr Hawter thinks Peacock's Walk would be ideal to accommodate businessmen who come over from the States to attend conferences in Brighton, and goodness knows there's a lot of those going on at present,' she added brightly. 'It couldn't be better. He's got the connections, and we've got the premises!'

'We're not going into partnership with him, are we?' queried Tony sceptically.

'Of course not!' exploded Jenny. 'I was only trying to explain to you that he does intend to keep Peacock's Walk as a hotel, and not,' she said accusingly, 'as a gambling casino, as you so gloomily predicted he might. Now are you satisfied?' she demanded.

Tony shrugged. 'I'd feel a great deal happier if the business wasn't being conducted by an agent. I'd like to see this Silas P. Hawter. Did he say when he was coming over—or if he was thinking of settling in this country?' he asked.

Jenny frowned at the question. 'Lots of Americans have businesses in this country,' she said patiently, 'but that doesn't mean that they have to reside here.' She shrugged. 'They do what he's apparently going to do, keep in close touch with the business. Usually they appoint a manager they can trust to run the business, but in our case, he's apparently satisfied enough to keep things running as they are. With the capital he can back us with, and the bookings he seems assured of, the place should go from strength to strength.' She gave him a beaming smile. 'But more than that, Tony, it means the staff will keep their jobs.'

Tony nodded complacently. 'Well, it looks like you've fallen on your feet, Goldie. Better make sure that those clauses of the staff being kept on are included in the contract—just in case,' he advised sternly.

With Tony apparently satisfied, however grudgingly he had given his approval, Jenny set about concluding the sale, and the contract with the necessary clauses inserted was signed six weeks later.

No more than a week after the signing and exchange of the contracts, a delighted Jenny received a communication from the new owner to the effect that she was to expect a party of fifteen business men from the States in ten days' time, two of whom would be bringing their secretaries. This number of guests was almost maximum to the amount the hotel could hold, for there were eighteen bedrooms, most of which had not been used for several months, and this left only one to be booked. Seeing the added footnote to say that she was to leave that booking open, Jenny did wonder whether Silas Hawter meant to accompany the party, but was not at the time of writing absolutely certain that he could make the trip—probably, she mused, through other business arrangements—but had taken the precaution of keeping the room free.

Jenny found herself hoping that he would make the trip, because she was now sure that that was his intention. The correspondence she had had with him to date had shown him to be a kindly, elderly man, and one she was sure she would be able to work very happily with for some time to come. It would also, she told herself, help to settle some of Tony's qualms; he had still not got used to the idea of working for someone he hadn't met, and she suspected the rest of the staff felt the same way. Her thoughts brightened yet further at the prospect of the activity she was about to set in motion when she related the news of the coming guests. For the past week, working under the orders of Mr Hawter, no bookings had been accepted, and the inactivity of the staff had produced a certain amount of speculation as to their future, in spite of Jenny's assurances that all was well, and as Jenny had walked through the deserted dining room, and the large empty lounge, she too knew a sense of uncertainty and could well understand their feelings.

On receipt of the news Jenny had to impart, the hotel became a hive of industry again. Rooms were springcleaned by willing, happy staff, and a general air of being in business again pervaded the atmosphere.

The ten days' notice that Jenny had at the time thought a little too long, and rather wished that only a few days' notice had been given of the coming bookings, flew by with a rapidity that amazed her. For not only the bedrooms received a thorough going over. The whole hotel came under the eagle eye of Dodie Hooney, and not a corner escaped her attention. The heavy velvet curtaining in the dining room and lounge, that might have done duty for another six months without cleaning, was taken down and replaced by new curtaining, the colour and texture being faithfully adhered to, for great care had always been taken to keep to the original old-world décor that so suited the dignified old building.

On the day before the arrival of the guests, Jenny did a tour of inspection, more to please Mrs Hooney than to satisfy herself that all was in order, and duly complimented the staff on their efforts when the tour was satisfactorily completed.

With a deep sense of satisfaction, she returned to her office and sat for a moment indulging in a little self-congratulatory musing. Peacock's Walk had come into its own again. The thought of Mark Chanter's reaction to the news that she had been successful, not only in her wish to keep the staff on, but had negotiated a sale resulting in an assured trade for the hotel, was an added bonus. The kind of business that he was so keen to promote, and was

sure to bring Peacock's Walk back into the top
bracket again, where it had once held pride of place.
No doubt that whoever it was that had passed the
previous information on to him would also pass on
the current state of affairs, and Jenny was a little
sorry that she would not be able to witness his fury
at losing out. He had been so sure of himself during
that last visit, and certain that she would have to
turn back to him, to, as he had put it, 'get you out of
the financial mess you've made of things'.

Her happy musings were abruptly curtailed at this
point by the arrival of the very man she had been
thinking about. She was too surprised by his sudden
appearance to notice that he had strolled into the
office without giving the customary knock, but when
the fact did sink in, she glared at him and remarked
coldly, 'I don't remember you asking to see me,'
and added for extra measure, 'I'm rather busy at the
moment, so if you don't mind ...' She left the sen-
tence unfinished, but she was sure he had got the
message.

Mark Chanter gave her a long considering look
before he drawled, 'Yes, aren't you. I've just popped
in to see that everything's in order.'

Jenny stared at him, then stated baldly, 'I don't
see what it's got to do with you. Would you mind
stating your business and leaving me to get on with
mine?'

Not bothering to answer this rather direct question, he further infuriated her by picking up the
printed menu forms for the week's fare. 'Seems
okay,' he remarked as he looked up to meet her

fuming eyes. 'Make sure you have plenty of melons on hand, will you? They're partial to them, I understand.'

Jenny gasped, and made an attempt to snatch the menus out of his hand, but was forestalled by his merely holding them up and out of her reach.

'Sit down, Miss Grange,' he commanded sternly. 'We're due for a little talk.'

Jenny knew better than to question his right in making such an order; she knew she would get nowhere by shouting and raving at him. Besides, it would be much more dignified to sit and glare at him—at least he would have to sit too, and she wouldn't have to stare up at him. She made her way towards her desk with as much dignity as she could muster, only to find her way barred and a pointing imperious finger directing her to take the chair in front of her desk.

'Sit there, will you? I'm not accustomed to holding slanging matches with my staff—I'll thank you to remember that in future.'

Jenny sat, simply because she had to. Her legs no longer proved reliable and felt decidedly wobbly. Her lips were stiff as she managed to get out, 'Would you mind explaining that last statement? Mr Hawter is my employer, and I've a contract to prove it,' she added on a firmer note.

Mark Chanter settled himself behind her desk before bothering to answer her, then giving a wry grimace remarked dryly, 'This chair is not for me,' and got up again and walked to where Malcolm's chair stood by the office window. Picking it up as if it were no weight at all, yet it was made of oak, he placed it in position behind the desk, pushing the lighter chair that Jenny had used back into the background.

Watching these movements, Jenny felt a sense of doom settling over her. His actions were somehow symbolic—as if he were saying, 'We've done with the past. The King is dead—long live the King!' She swallowed as her wide eyes met his implacable ones.

'Now where were we?' he asked casually, and gave a mock frown of concentration. 'Ah, yes, the contract.' He gave her a grin that Jenny could only describe as wolfish, and she felt a prickly sensation along her spine. 'Silas P. Hawter,' he went on slowly, taking his time, and savouring with no little pleasure her wide eyes and white face, 'is the name of a company of which I hold a majority of shares.' He nodded slowly as Jenny attempted to intervene. 'Yes, there is a Silas P. Hawter. He was the original owner of the company, but he has since sold out. He still remains interested in the company, of course, and watches over our interests in the States, purely on an advisory basis.'

Jenny gasped as the implication hit her. Of all the low-down tricks! He couldn't have been honest about it from the start, could he? Oh, no, she thought bitterly—he knew she wouldn't have entertained another bid from him for Peacock's Walk— not if she could have got someone else! 'I suppose the older staff will now get their marching orders,' she commented bitterly. 'At least you were honest about that when you came to see me,' she added in a low voice.

He did not answer her for a second or so, and when Jenny glanced up at him she was surprised by the flash of fury in his eyes. 'The contract states that all staff are to be retained, if I remember rightly,' he said savagely. 'I made a concession there for which you ought to be grateful.'

Grateful! Jenny wanted to shout the word at him. She'd be grateful if he left her alone. He had enough hotels, didn't he? Why should he want Peacock's Walk? 'Thank you,' she managed to get out between clenched teeth.

'Will it be so repugnant working for me?' he asked softly, yet goadingly. 'It won't be so very different from the job you used to have with Peacock —er—workwise, that is. There won't be any business trips, I'm afraid,' he added meaningly. 'We've got that side of it over with, haven't we?'

Jenny's small hands clenched into fists. He didn't have to bring that up to make sure she understood the position. She did not answer. There was nothing she could say anyway, nothing that he would understand.

'I'm not,' he went on smoothly, 'saying that time won't alter the situation.'

Jenny's eyes had been centred on her hands, but now they flew to his, and the incredulity in hers made him smile again. She didn't care for that smile any more than she had cared for the other one he had given her, or the way his narrowed eyes were studying her slight figure.

'You're a very attractive woman, Jenny,' he said softly. 'I might just decide to kick over the traces with you.' He gave a nonchalant shrug as he added meaningly, 'Who knows?'

Her eyes never left his face, even though she felt the flush spread over her features. There was nothing like putting it on the line, she thought furiously. It wasn't enough for him to make her feel cheap, he had to emphasize the fact that he thought her a go-getter as well, and had the temerity to dangle a golden carrot in front of her!

Jenny sent a silent thank-you to Malcolm for leaving her some security. He had been right about Mark Chanter—he did use women as playthings, she thought scathingly; if she had ever needed proof of this, then she had just received it. She could, and would, get out. The staff were taken care of, so there was no worry there. Her head was held high as she replied steadily, 'I'm afraid I have no wish to resurrect the past. I'm flattered, of course, by your remarks.' Her lovely eyes glinted with green sparks as she added significantly, 'I didn't enjoy the last chapter in our romantic skirmish, so I'll pass this time, if you don't mind.'

For one frightening moment it looked as if he would yank her out of her chair, but her beating heart calmed when she saw him sit down again slowly, but his eyes never left hers as he said softly, 'You rather underrated me, didn't you? But time will teach you not to make the same mistake again. Who's the current fancy?' he shot out at her.

Jenny stared at him and almost gasped at his

audacity. She could speak the truth and say there
was no one, but on second thoughts he might leave
her alone if there was someone else in the running.
This thought, however, was soon replaced by the
certain surety that he knew very well that there was
no one; she had made sure of that by rebuffing any
would-be suitors. 'I don't see that that's any of your
business,' she contented herself with.

'Ah, but I do want my staff to be happy,' he replied smoothly. 'I'm rather partial to the personal
approach, you know. It makes for good relations all
round.'

'I'm sure that whoever takes over from me will
be happy to know that,' Jenny got out, willing herself to stay calm. 'I presume it is the secretarial
position you had in mind for me?' She paused at
the look of mockery in his eyes as she said this and
could guess his thoughts. A feeling of complete helplessness passed over her, and with it a wish to hit
back hard and hurt this man as much as he had
hurt her. It was a feeling totally alien to her nature,
bringing a lost, uncertain backlash in its wake. All
her previous values had disappeared in a puff of
smoke. She had never hurt anyone before, at least,
not consciously so, but just give her a chance to get
her own back on this man and she would jump at
it! 'I only agreed to stay on because Mr Hawter
specifically asked me to,' she resumed slowly. 'At
your direction, I suppose?' she asked in a tight hard
voice, the dislike she felt for him plainly visible in
her eyes as she looked at him.

He gave her a complacent nod, as if to say she

ought to have known this, and Jenny received an inner sense of shock as she digested the fact that her open hostility towards him did not infuriate him; if anything it seemed to cause him some gratification, and she was doubly grateful to providence that she was not dependent in any way on him, because there would be precious little understanding between them.

'You wanted all the staff retained,' he answered smoothly. 'Under those conditions I deemed it wiser to keep you on as well. It might have caused a few difficulties otherwise.' He gave her a speculative look. 'They're very attached to you, aren't they?' he observed caustically.

Jenny privately conceded this point, although it was only the older staff who felt they owed allegiance to her, and it was they who held the most responsible positions in the hotel. Looking at it from that point of view it made sense. Even so, Mark must have known what her reaction would have been when she found out that he owned the hotel. It struck her that he had gone to a lot of trouble to ensure the smooth running of the hotel, and she wondered why. It was not as if he couldn't replace any member of staff at a day's notice; he had enough hotel staff at his command to cover any such vacancies—including secretarial staff, she thought scathingly.

'I'm sure,' he went on carefully, 'that when you think things over, you will retract what I presume to be your notice. You signed a contract, remember, and if you fail to honour it, I am under no obliga-

tion to fulfil my part of it. In other words, Miss
Grange, if you go, so does the rest of the staff, and I
shall return to my original plans in keeping such
staff as I think suitable for the work entailed.'

The indignation Jenny felt at this pompous ulti-
matum was soon replaced by a dawning realisation
of the clever tactics now being used on her—and she
had very nearly fallen for it! He had quite deliberately riled her into reacting in just the way she had
reacted. He knew she didn't need the money, so the
job was not essential to her, and had taken great
pains to outline the future for her as his secretary
—for she would be his secretary; no manager would
be appointed here, as was the usual procedure in
his other hotels, instinctively she was certain of this,
just as surely as she was now certain of the reason
why he had insisted on retaining her. It was simple
really, and she ought to have seen it coming. Tony,
she thought sadly, hadn't been all that far wrong
when he had said she couldn't see the wood for the
trees. She drew in a deep breath—it wasn't a wood,
it was a great forest—no, forest wasn't the right
definition, more akin to a jungle where the tiger
stalked its prey. The tiger was sitting right in front
of her, waiting to pounce at any given moment. She
shivered at the thought, and told herself she was
being fanciful.

She looked back at him and found, as she had expected, that he was watching her closely, waiting for
her to throw the job in his face regardless of the
consequences of her actions. He would assume that
her pride would force her to leave, but he didn't

really know her—he never had. Pride was something she could do without when it concerned the welfare of the people she loved. It was her pride that Mark had gambled on—a ploy that would have worked with anyone else, herself included, if it hadn't concerned others.

There was a little consolation for her in the fact that he was about to find that his strategy in getting rid of not only her, but the older staff that he had not wanted to keep on, had suffered a severe setback.

Her head was held high as her wide grey-green eyes met his hard grey stare unflinchingly as she replied haughtily, 'It seems I must thank you for reminding me of my responsibilities. Under the circumstances, I have no option but to stay on.'

Her gaze remained fixed on his face, hoping to witness the fury this decision brought, but there was no alteration in his expression, although when he answered, Jenny caught a hint of mockery in his eyes—a challenge maybe? she wondered. Her lips set in a firm line. He could be as obnoxious as he liked, it wouldn't get him anywhere. She was not as soft as she had been two years ago, and if he dared to even attempt to 'kick over the traces' as he had put it, with her, then he would soon be acquainted of this fact.

As if sensing her thought, he said softly, 'Don't worry, I'm not short of feminine company at the moment.'

To her fury, Jenny felt herself flush, and to cover her confusion, she snapped out, 'Are there any other arrangements you'd like made?' adding meaningly, 'for our guests.'

Mark Chanter's mouth quirked slightly at the corners, as if regretting the sudden change of conversation. 'It all seems in order,' he remarked dryly, 'for which you have my congratulations. I like you like that,' he shot out at her, catching her unawares as she made a few notes on the notepad she had picked up ready to resume her secretarial duties.

Her flush deepened as she replied caustically, 'As you once said, I am a good secretary and will, I hope, continue to be, in spite of the changed circumstances. One thing I would ask you to bear in mind, and that is that our relationship should remain a business one. Nothing else is sought, or indeed, wanted.'

Mark's eyes narrowed at this, and he replied harshly, 'Aren't you meeting your fences a little early? I'm not likely to make the same mistake again, if that's what you're referring to.' His glance flickered over her, taking in her soft cashmere sweater of a shade of green that highlighted her eyes, and passed on from her neatly tailored grey skirt to her shapely nyloned legs and her small feet encased in grey moccasins. 'Peacock must have had quite a lot going for him where you were concerned,' he added pointedly, 'but the perks helped too, didn't they? One mustn't forget that. At least you know where you are with me. I'm not likely to add to that little nest egg he left you. Yes, Miss Grange—ours will be a business relationship, and don't go back to the clinging vine type, will you? In case you're ever tempted to do so in the future, I've gone off that act.'

He pointed to the chair from which Jenny had risen before making her way towards the door. She didn't have to stand this kind of barbed torture; he said he had nothing else for her to make a note of, and she saw no reason to stay. 'Sit down, please, I haven't finished. You really must remember who's calling the tune now, and this is business,' he added harshly. 'It was you who brought the personal angle into the limelight, remember. Now that we've got that straight, there's a few other things I wanted to discuss with you, such as future policies. Peacock's Walk is now under Chanter Administration and there are certain rules I shall expect adhered to.'

It was no easy task for Jenny to concentrate on the rules he was reeling out to her, let alone keep the notebook steady in her trembling hands, but she somehow managed it, and hoped her concentration, now centred on the page she was covering with her neat shorthand, would hide the conflict raging inside her, willing herself to remember the reason why she had accepted the job, and as unpalatable as it was obviously going to be, why she had to see it through.

CHAPTER THREE

A SHORT while after Mark had left her, Jenny sat alone in the office that had once been her domain, but would from now on be shared, if that was the right word, she thought unhappily, with the august person of Mark Chanter. That he expected her to revert to her original role, to not only take over the secretarial duties but to share the same office as her boss, as she had done with Malcolm, he had left her in no doubt by obliquely remarking that he presumed the other desk was about somewhere, and would she arrange to have it reinstated back to its previous position.

This meant having a word with Rose, for the desk had been allotted to reception shortly after Jenny had taken over the running of the hotel. At this thought she winced, for it brought to mind the next worry on her agenda—that of telling the staff that they were now part of the Chanter group, and posting up a list of the rules they would now be expected to adhere to.

Hard on the heels of this miserable thought came another one even more unpalatable than the last one. Tony had to be told of the identity of the new owner of Peacock's Walk, and then Dodie would have to be put into the picture. She swallowed as she envisaged Dodie's amazed reaction at the news she had to impart to her.

Of Tony's reaction she hardly dared think! He could, and very probably would, take her to task for not foreseeing what had happened, although how she could have done was beyond her present reasoning.

It did not occur to her that the delicate task of explaining the position to the staff would be carried out by the man himself, and when thinking about it afterwards, Jenny ought to have known this. He did not believe in delegating such responsibilities to others. The staff were now under his direction, and he lost no time in enlightening them on this fact.

This was related to Jenny by a scowling Tony, who joined her just before lunch as she was still debating whether she ought to call a meeting of staff, or whether to see them individually, and in the case of the older staff, reassure them that their jobs were not at risk and that they would keep the positions they held. She had just decided on the latter course, when Tony stalked into the office after giving a short perfunctory knock.

'I've just attended a very enlightening meeting in the staff room,' he said without preamble. 'Called by one Mark Chanter,' he added significantly, and gave the startled Jenny a curt nod. 'Said it was too pat, didn't I?' he tacked on sourly.

Jenny looked away quickly, waiting for the sermon she was sure she was about to receive, and was a little surprised when nothing else was said. As she watched him perch himself in his favourite position on the corner of the desk, the thought went through her mind that he wouldn't ever get the opportunity of doing that again. She couldn't see the new owner of Peacock's Walk accepting what he would term as familiarity from the members of staff, in spite of his earlier assertion of wanting the staff to be happy and believing in the personal approach.

Tony's gloomy acceptance of the situation made her feel worse. She would have felt much better if he had lectured her, for she had, as he had said not very long ago, thrown her hat over the windmill with a vengeance, and there was no retrieving it.

She looked down at her hands. 'As usual, you were right,' she said in a low voice. 'I took everything at face value, didn't I? And it's too late to back out now.' She looked back at Tony, who was studying her closely with a worried expression in his eyes. 'I'm sorry, Tony, I ought to have made more enquiries. You did warn me.' She shrugged her slim shoulders. 'I was so sure I was doing the right thing,' she ended miserably.

'Wouldn't have done any good if you had made enquiries,' he said dolefully. 'You'd only have found out what Mark Chanter wanted you to find out. The Company's registered in America. Enquiries this end wouldn't have helped, would they?'

Jenny grinned weakly at his stout attempt to make her feel better.

'Why did he change his mind about keeping all

the staff on?' he asked her suddenly, trying to sound offhanded, but Jenny knew better. Like Dodie, he was trying to find out how this affected her, and she saw no reason why she shouldn't put him in the picture. He had to know some time, and to mislead him now would cause a lot of complications later.

'Because he knew I wouldn't sell otherwise,' she said slowly. 'I told him that when he made the first offer, remember? He also,' she went on hoping her voice did not show the depression she felt, 'thought it would be a good idea if I stayed on as well.'

'Did he?' growled Tony. 'I hope you put him right on that score. From what he said at that meeting, I gather he intends to favour us with his presence for some time to come.' He gave Jenny a searching look. 'And where does that leave you?' he demanded.

Jenny drew in a deep breath. 'Right where I came in,' she answered slowly, 'doing secretarial work.'

'His secretary?' Tony asked with raised brows, and as she nodded confirmatively, he exploded, 'Well, he's got a nerve! Not that I'm all that surprised, mind you,' he hinted darkly. 'No doubt he hopes to take on from where he thought Malcolm left off.'

This was so near the truth that Jenny couldn't help giving him a startled stare, and this confirmed his suspicions. He leant towards her and wagged an admonishing finger at her. 'If you know what's good for you, you'll go right to your rooms and pack,' he advised her sternly. 'I'm giving you the sort of ad-

vice your father would have given you,' he added
grimly. 'Note my words, Mark Chanter mightn't
want marriage, but he's no objection to the perks
that go with it.'

'Tony!' gasped a red-cheeked Jenny. 'It wasn't
like that at all—and well you know it!'

'I know it,' answered Tony, 'but he didn't. And
that's precisely how he sees things.'

Jenny's flush died down and she gave him a
curious look. 'Why do you hate him so much,
Tony?' she asked quietly.

He shrugged expressively. 'I loathe all playboys,'
he said sourly. 'Have everything handed to them on
a plate—education, the lot, and they get to expect
things to drop into their laps from the skies. He's
no different from the rest.' He gave her a sharp
look. 'It's my belief he's come back for a second bite
at the cherry, and you're no match for him. It must
have been galling for him with his looks and money
to get as far as putting a ring on your finger, only
to find himself pipped at the post by his friend, and
a man like that doesn't forget the past. His pride
wouldn't allow it.'

His expression softened as it rested on Jenny,
who was looking down at her hands. 'I'll tell you
something else, too,' he added gently. 'If a vote was
put to the staff right now on whether you ought to
stay on, the answer would be a deafening no—they
saw what happened. It took us a year to get that
shellshocked look out of your eyes—we haven't forgotten either!'

Jenny's eyes glistened as she looked up at him

and replied, 'You've forgotten Malcolm, Tony. It all happened at the same time, remember?'

Tony shook his head adamantly. 'That wasn't the way we saw it,' he muttered. 'And we'd all feel a lot easier if you walked out of the job.'

With a sigh that told Tony that he was on a losing streak, Jenny gave a wry smile. 'I know you won't believe this,' she began firmly, 'but I'm in no danger whatsoever of "going soft", as you put it, over Mark Chanter again. Furthermore,' she added with a glint in her eye, 'I simply don't see why I should give him the opportunity of getting rid of the staff he didn't want to employ.' She flung him a challenging look. 'In spite of what you think, Tony, he wants me out—so I'm afraid your notion of amorous intent doesn't hold water. He wanted me to throw the job in his face and walk out—but I didn't oblige him—not when I realised the purpose behind the offer.'

Her small hands clenched as she added staunchly, 'So I stay, and so do the others. I'm not,' she got in quickly as Tony started to interrupt her, 'being a martyr. I know you and Dodie have something to fall back on if the worst comes to the worst, but Thomas and Flo James haven't—neither has Boots. I intend to stay put until we've found them alternative work elsewhere—and when that's done, then I'll walk out gladly, so you can tell them that. I don't suppose any of them will be too keen on staying anyway—not if they feel the same way as you do about things, but I'm not leaving until they have another job to go to.' Her chin lifted defiantly,

'We go in our own good time, Tony—not in his.'

With this stout declaration, Tony had to accept defeat, but was not at all happy with the situation. He left her shortly afterwards muttering something about getting on to friends of his in the trade who might know of a few vacancies suitable for their requirements. As for himself, he reminded Jenny of her earlier suggestion of opening a restaurant somewhere, and said the idea had been a good one and he would make a few enquiries in that direction.

There was a hint of tears in her eyes as she gazed at the closed door after he had left her. He was making sure he kept an eye on her, she thought. She would be given no time to mope, Tony would see to that, and although she was grateful, she did wish he would realise that she was old enough to look out for herself now. On this thought she sighed. Old habits die hard. If it wasn't Tony fussing over her, it would be Dodie, so she might as well accept their protectiveness for what it was, a sincere wish for her happiness—just that, and nothing more.

The following morning Jenny was surprised to find her desk in position in the corner of the large office, complete with typewriter—just as it had been in Malcolm's time, particularly as she had omitted to ask Rose for its return the day before, and her cheeks tinged pink when she realised that Mark had made certain that she fulfilled her duties forthwith by personally attending to the matter. A deeper pink suffused her cheeks when she thought of Rose's reaction to the news that Jenny had become his secretary.

With a slight exclamation of annoyance, Jenny took her place behind her desk. He couldn't even leave her to see to her end of things, could he? Oh, no, not he! It would be his way of showing her who was in charge now—and not only her—the rest of the staff too! Her small even teeth caught her lower lip as she remembered what Tony had said about Mark Chanter intending to be around for quite some time. As long, she thought bitterly, as it took for him to gain his objective and remove her and the rest of the unwanted staff from Peacock's Walk.

A quick perusal of the desk drawers confirmed that all her personal belongings had been removed from the large desk to her small one, and gazing over to the large desk that had once been hers, she saw that a framed photograph had been placed on the desk, together with the usual items of office equipment.

Pushing aside the natural instinct to go over to the desk and look at whoever had been so honoured as to rate such a position in her new employer's life, she settled down to await his arrival, willing herself to remain calm and businesslike, no matter how much provocation she received, for she had no doubt in her mind that he intended to be as objectionable as possible, and she would never forgive herself if she allowed him to reach his objective.

On hearing the deep chimes of the lounge clock that announced that it was nine o'clock, she shifted restlessly in her chair. It was time that he put in an appearance, she thought. It was not as if he had far to come, for he had taken the vacant room that Jenny had misguidedly thought that Silas Hawter had reserved for himself. This she had learnt from Dodie the previous evening—that, and a few other things, that added up to the same sort of lecture given her by Tony, and she had had to repeat what she had told Tony—that she would go in her own good time—and not before.

A quick glance at her watch told her that it was now ten minutes past the hour, and still no sign of Mark Chanter. Her lips firmed on the thought that perhaps this was an intended lapse on his part to keep her waiting. It was also probable that he was taking a last look around the hotel, because this was the day that the American guests were due. Even so, she thought bleakly, he had already satisfied himself on this point the day before, and there was no need for another inspection.

With her elbows on her desk and her face cupped in her hands, Jenny had to concede that she did not know very much about Mark Chanter—business-wise, that was, but in all fairness she knew he did not warrant the 'playboy' charge that Tony had levelled against him. Although Malcolm's friendship with Mark had turned to emnity because of Mark's interest in her, Malcolm had always respected Mark's business acumen, and had sought his advice on many occasions in the past. Not every business handed down from father to son flourished so successfully as Chanter Enterprises had—not without a certain amount of hard work, for what was once a moderately successful hotel had become one of many.

At nine-fifteen, Jenny rang through to reception, and trying to keep the annoyance she felt at having to seek information on her new boss's movements, asked Rose if she had seen anything of Mr Chanter.

Rose gave a chatty, 'Oh, he's out, Miss Grange. I only know because I met him on his way out when I arrived.' There was a short pause before she added helpfully, 'Perhaps something came up. He didn't leave any message that I know of.'

Jenny thanked her and replaced the receiver carefully, only just managing not to slam it down. It was not Rose's fault that Mark Chanter had not seen fit to advise them of his movements.

Her baleful look left the receiver and swept over the desk, for she had to use the phone on Mark's desk as it was the only one in the room. Her glare rested on the back of the photograph in front of her, and without a second thought she turned it towards her, fully expecting to see the face of some anonymous beauty that had caught his eye. Her eyes widened in surprise as she stared at her own image.

Her surprise soon gave way to incredulity, then puzzlement, for she well remembered when the photograph had been taken, and the occasion. It had been taken by Malcolm, who had caught her laughing at some quip made by her father during an inspection of part of the hotel grounds that Malcolm had in mind to use for the building of a few chalets, to cope with the overflow of guests during the peak season.

Jenny's frown deepened as she replaced the photograph with hands that trembled slightly. The snap had been such a good one that Malcolm had had an enlargement made, and as far as Jenny knew, it had remained his property. She simply could not see Malcolm giving it to Mark, even though the snap had been taken a year before she met Mark.

As she did not know the answer, or the reason why he should have the photograph in such a prominent position, she pushed the disturbing question out of her mind for the time being, and dwelt on the memories the photograph had evoked.

There had been no clouds on her horizon then, and no Prince Charming, as she had once regarded Mark Chanter. Her existence had been one of calm acceptance and happiness—for she had been happy, she thought wistfully. Malcolm had never seemed an employer to either her father or her, for he had grown up with Jenny, and in many ways had been closer to Mr Grange than to his own father, who, inclined to rheumatics, had been a follower of the sun, and had hated the damp English climate.

Her gaze went back to the laughing girl in the photograph, who now seemed a stranger to her. It was hard to imagine that she had once been as gay and as carefree as that picture depicted. She sighed on the thought that less than two years after the photograph had been taken she had lost not only her father, but Malcolm too.

After the loss of two such dear people in her life, Jenny thought she had the answer as to why Mark Chanter had failed to capture her heart. She had nothing more to give; all emotion had been drained out of her before a lasting link had been formed. It had been a wonderful, exhilarating period in her life while the attraction had lasted, but she had always had the curious feeling that she would have to wake up some time, and the death of her father had been the forerunner of her awakening.

Jenny had never known exactly what her father had thought of Mark. He had always made him very welcome, as indeed he had done to any of Malcolm's friends. All she did know was that if he had not thought him a suitable partner for his daughter, he would have said so, for as kindly as he was, he would not have held his peace on this issue, and Jenny could only assume that he approved of him. This was a point in Mark's favour, for her father had been an astute man. It had since occurred to Jenny to wonder if her father had known of Malcolm's feelings for her, and she had come to the conclusion that he had known, for there was very little that he missed, in spite of his quiet unassuming nature.

With an impatient movement she turned the photograph back to its original position so that the back of the frame was now presented to her, and her gaze swept over the contents of the large desk. It was then that her eye caught a tape that had been left in the centre of the desk, and under it a note. She drew in a breath of sheer exasperation; how stupid of her! She ought to have thought of looking before, but it hadn't occurred to her, and if she had not satisfied her curiosity over the identity of the subject in the photograph, she wouldn't have found the tape, for two large wire trays for correspondence blocked her view from the front of the desk.

The thought that Mark had known that she would not be able to resist looking at the photograph gave her a few bad moments, but, she argued silently with herself, she would not have bothered to look at it if she hadn't had to use the telephone on his desk—but he wouldn't have thought of that, she told herself bitterly as she picked up the tape and read the instructions on the note that had been placed under it.

The instructions were brief and to the point, and an added postscript told her that he would be back shortly after midday, accompanied by their American guests.

For the rest of that morning Jenny threw herself into her work, refusing to be lulled back into memory lane by that persuasive, smooth voice of Mark's, but her cheeks flamed pink at an added soft reminder of his at the end of the second letter on the tape that she must remind him to have a bottle of Advocaat sent up to his room, and his dry, 'I presume you still have the same preference for it,' made her fingers freeze on the typewriter keys. She was not absolutely sure that he was referring to her, as it did occur to her that he might have originally meant the tape to be transcribed by his personal secretary, although there was no denying that she did prefer the drink he had mentioned.

As her fingers flew over the keys at the start of

another letter, she told herself that that was one instruction she would definitely not be carrying out! Mark might be in the habit of entertaining his secretary in his private rooms at his other hotels, but he was in for a disappointment if he hoped for the same arrangement with her.

To think she might have married such a man, she thought indignantly. Tony hadn't been so far off the mark at that. The man was a womaniser! The sooner she got out, the better!

When Tony rang her shortly afterwards, telling her that it looked as if he had managed to find a position for Boots at one of the smaller guest houses in Brighton, she felt a surge of relief flow through her. One down and two to go, she thought cheerfully, although it was a great pity that they couldn't all walk out en bloc—not that this happening would cause Mark Chanter any grief—if anything, joy, she thought shrewdly, but it would give her great satisfaction nevertheless.

The American delegates invaded the premises shortly after midday, and Jenny, hearing the by now familiar accents floating up to her office window from the hotel entrance below, felt a glow of pride at the unrestrained comments of their approval of the chosen quarters for their stay while attending the conference.

When she had owned the hotel, it would have been her policy to go down and greet her guests, now, as secretary, she stayed where she was, feeling in an odd way a little relieved that she no longer need play a major role in the business. It was rather pleasant to sit back and let someone else do the worrying and fussing over the comfort of their guests, and be able to remain a nonentity in the background.

With these thoughts in mind, she was a little nonplussed when Mark strode into the office a few minutes later accompanied by an elderly, plump man, to whom Mark blithely introduced her with a, 'This is Jenny Grange, Silas,' and turning to Jenny, added blandly, 'Mr Hawter insisted on meeting you at the earliest opportunity.'

Jenny shook hands with Silas Hawter, and tried hard to look impersonal about it. It was an effort not to snub him, for this was the man who had helped Mark engineer the acquisition of the hotel. That Mark Chanter had had the effrontery to carry out the introduction did not surprise her one bit, but she did wonder why he had bothered.

'A pleasure to meet you,' enthused Mr Hawter, and Jenny fervently wished she could say the same, but in all honesty she could not, but just listened as the jolly, plump man rambled on with the same enthusiasm. 'Mark said you were special—and I can see why,' he remarked as his homely face broke into a wide smile.

Jenny's features froze on this comment, and her furious eyes met Mark's bland ones. 'I'm flattered by Mr Chanter's remarks,' she bit out furiously, unable to remain impersonal any longer. 'And I'm sure he feels the same way about the rest of the staff,' she added waspishly, and coloured as Mark broke in with a swift, 'Now I wouldn't go as far as to say that,' reply, accompanied by a wicked grin.

When Jenny had managed to disentangle her hand from Mr Hawter's firm shake, she saw with no little consternation a look pass from him to Mark, a look that had conspiracy written all over it, and she longed to shout at them that she hoped they were satisfied with themselves at the way they had hoodwinked her into selling Peacock's Walk to Chanter Enterprises. With a supreme effort she managed to hold her peace. The thing was done now, and no amount of hoping would alter the situation, and the thought of the older staff helped her to reply to Silas Hawter's unexpected invitation to her to join him at dinner that evening, and while she was tempted to find an excuse, the apologetic look he sent Mark as he made the request made Jenny accept without hesitation, if only to show him that her private life was no concern of Mark Chanter's. Whatever delusions Silas Hawter was suffering from regarding the exact relationship between her and Mark would soon be put to rights after a little chat over the dinner table.

A little before eight that evening, Jenny made her way to the hotel restaurant for her dinner date with Silas Hawter. Wearing an off-the-shoulder green velvet gown that highlighted her fair hair and brought out the green lights in her eyes, she threaded her way past the other diners, towards the table at the end of the room that had been reserved for her host.

It was with no little appreciation that she observed the frankly admiring looks she received from

the occupants of the other tables. She had wanted
to look her best and had gone to some pains to
achieve the resultant effect, and now felt quite justi-
fied for her trouble. It was not often that Jenny
bothered to dress up for any occasion. In fact, not
since Mark had gone out of her life, and this had
not been for any other reason than for a wish to
remain in the background as much as possible, and
not, as Tony and the rest of the staff had thought at
that time, because Mark had jilted her.

As she passed the table next to the one she was
heading for, she met Mark's mocking eyes with a
glint of defiance in hers, and she didn't know why
she should choose this particular time to remember
that he had not liked her hair twisted up on top of
her head as she had chosen to style it that evening,
but she was extremely grateful that she had just happened to put it up, more from a wish to look older
and more sophisticated than she felt.

A light flush stained her cheeks, as she heard
Mark murmur in a low voice as she floated past
him, 'You look gorgeous, kitten, but don't overdo
the welcome, will you?'

Once again she caught the proprietorial note in
his voice; he might just as well have said, 'I shall
be watching you, so keep it cool,' and she couldn't
understand his reasoning at all. He had Peacock's
Walk, and nothing she said or did would change
the situation, so why he had to act the big brother
was beyond her. Unless, a tiny voice whispered inside her, he did intend to take over where Malcolm
had left off, as Tony had intimated earlier, in which

case, she thought indignantly, he had a few surprises in store, not to mention disappointments!

Her host more or less echoed Mark's sentiments —as far as her appearance went, that was—and seated her with courtly, old-fashioned etiquette that was somehow touching, and made her feel like weeping, for her father had possessed the same courteousness towards his guests, and it was something that was sadly lacking in up-to-date mannerisms.

It was the same with the ordering of the meal, for after ascertaining her likes and dislikes, Silas made the selection, and Jenny had only to sit back and silently approve of his choice of fare. While they waited for the first course to be served, Silas poured her a glass of a white Sauternes that he told her he could thoroughly recommend, and took his time slowly sipping his drink before coming to the subject Jenny shrewdly guessed had been the reason for his invitation.

'I guess,' he began after a few moments' deliberation, 'I owe you an apology, Miss Grange,' and looked up to meet Jenny's wary glance at him. 'But first,' he went on as he placed his glass down on the table, 'I must thank you for receiving me as you did earlier on. I wouldn't have been a bit surprised if you'd refused to meet me,' he gave a quick grin as a thought struck him at this point, and added dryly, 'Not that Mark gave you much choice in the matter, I admit, but you could have given me the cold shoulder, and I'm right grateful that you didn't.'

Jenny looked down at the table, for she knew she

hardly deserved such a tribute. If it had not been
for the thought of the staff she might well have given
him the 'cold shoulder', as he had so aptly put it. As
it was, she had had to exercise a great deal of self-
control not to give her thoughts away, although
his apology told her that he was not insensible of her
feelings in this.

'Mark told me he'd been unsuccessful in his
earlier bid,' Silas went on carefully, and gave a slight
shrug. 'Normally, one would put this down to the
one that got away—you can't win 'em all, as you'd
say, but there were certain reasons why I wanted
him to have this place.'

Jenny was grateful for the intervention of the
waiter just then, for she was wondering if he knew
the history behind Mark's interest in the hotel, as
she had come to the undeniable conclusion that
Tony had been right all along in his summing-up
of her ex-fiancé's motives in purchasing Peacock's
Walk. His subtle warning to her had ended all
speculation on this front, and was intended to give
Jenny due notice of his renewed interest in her.
It also gave her time to reinforce her battlements.

Nothing more was said until they had finished
the starters, and as Jenny's spoon dipped into her
avocado vinaigrette, she wondered if Silas Hawter
had come as Mark's champion. If so, it was a wasted
journey. Somehow she must convey this to him,
but as Mark's friend he was not likely to hear anything against him, not that she intended to rake up
the past, that was between Mark and herself, and
no one else.

'I've known Mark for a very long time,' began Silas ruminatively, while they waited for the first course to be served, 'both as a friend and a business colleague. As a friend, I owe him quite a lot—he saved me from making an all time fool of myself not so very long ago.' He gave Jenny a sheepish grin. 'Oh, I know I ought to have known better than to have entered into the romantic stakes at my age, and I didn't appreciate his advice at the time, but I was sure thankful that I acted upon it later. The woman was a confidence trickster and had me all trussed up for plucking until Mark arrived on the scene.' He shot Jenny a keen glance as he added dryly, 'That was one man she didn't fool—no, sir! Although there'd been plenty of others. I'd back his judgment all the way, no matter what the situation.'

Jenny sat silent, although there was a lot she could have added to his somewhat sweeping statement about Mark's astuteness. In her case, his reasoning power appeared to have come unstuck— or perhaps it hadn't, she thought dryly. Any excuse was better than none when one wanted to get out from under, as she was sure he had when he had wanted to end the engagement.

Silas's enthusiastic comments on the appetisingly prepared blue trout that was placed before them a few seconds later brought her out of her musings. 'If that tastes half as good as it looks, I can see I shall be sending the chef my compliments,' he said happily, as he added a few garnishings to Jenny's plate, only stopping when she indicated that she had enough.

The trout and the course that followed, came well up to expectation, as Jenny had known it would, and the conversation lagged until full justice had been done to Tony's culinary efforts, but all too soon for Jenny's liking they were back to the subject she least wanted to discuss.

'As fond as I am of that boy,' began Silas as he lit a cigar and puffed contentedly away at it. 'I want him settled back in England. There's Dilys, you see,' he said, as he refilled Jenny's glass before she could stop him. 'Er . . . she's my niece,' he explained. 'She's got what I believe is called a "hang-up" on Mark.' He pursed his lips gently. 'Now I'm as fond of Dilys as any man would be of his only brother's daughter —more so—particularly as my brother died when she was twelve. Her mother remarried some years later, but Dilys never really took to her stepfather, and consequently she's lived with me since then. In a sense, she's more of a daughter to me than a niece,' he hesitated a short while before he added significantly, 'and Mark's hung-up on you—so I guess I want to see things straightened out this end, one way or the other—not only for Dilys's sake, but for Mark's, too.'

Jenny's eyes opened wide in astonishment at this calm statement. For goodness' sake, what had Mark told him? Had he used her as an excuse for not getting involved with the unfortunate Dilys? It was all she could do not to turn round and see what Mark was making of the cosy chat she was having with his friend, and would dearly have liked to call him over and confront him with the absurd delusion Silas Hawter was labouring under. On recalling the wicked look in his eye when she had answered his comment on her being 'special', she decided to let well alone. This was something she had to handle on her own.

Her wide eyes met Silas Hawter's earnest brown ones, and something in his expression stopped her from uttering a sharp 'Stuff and nonsense!' and made her remember that he had aided and abetted Mark Chanter for the simple reason that he loved his niece, and Jenny had no quarrel with that sentiment. As for Mark—if Silas Hawter's niece was anything like her uncle in character, she deserved someone better than Mark—although there was no accounting for tastes, she thought sadly.

'You've not got your facts right,' she said gently. 'I don't know what Mark has told you about our association, but in spite of the fact that we were once engaged—an engagement, I might add, that he broke off, there is absolutely nothing between us now. In point of fact,' she went on firmly, 'I hadn't set eyes on him for two years until he came to Peacock's Walk to make an offer.'

She smiled at Silas as she added, 'I'm afraid you'll have to look elsewhere if you want to find the reason behind his tardiness in getting involved with your niece. Has it occurred to you,' she asked suddenly, seeing no reason why she shouldn't say exactly what she thought on the matter, 'that there are some men who shy at marriage? My opinion, for what it's

worth, is that Mark Chanter is one of those men.'
She shrugged her slim shoulders as she added, 'It
does rather curb their activities, you know, particularly when they're as popular with the opposite
sex as he is.' The added rider came out on a wasp-
ish note, and rather surprised Jenny, since she
hadn't meant it to sound as if she was bitter.

Silas Hawter nodded his head gently, as if he had
received confirmation of some kind—of what, Jenny
had no idea until he spoke. 'He hurt you a lot,
didn't he?' he said in a low voice.

Jenny gave an exasperated sigh as she replied
quickly, 'As a matter of fact, he didn't.' She pushed
back a stray wisp of hair that had clung to her forehead in a movement that showed her impatience
with the situation. 'Oh, dear, I haven't explained
how it was very clearly, have I?' She was silent
while she marshalled her thoughts to try again and
put the facts before him in a way that he would
understand, but before she could start again, Silas
broke in with, 'Would you mind very much telling
me why he broke off the engagement?'

Jenny frowned and pulled her thoughts away
from the explanation she was preparing to give him.
It was as good a way as any, she thought as she
answered lightly, 'I could say it was because he lost
interest, and I wouldn't be telling a lie, but as
you're bound to hear the other side of it, I might
as well tell you the facts leading up to the ending
of the engagement. To put it bluntly, he thought I
was having an affair with Malcolm Peacock. Malcolm owned Peacock's Walk, I was his secretary.

When Malcolm was killed in a car crash, I was his beneficiary. It was all Mark needed for proof, and he took full advantage of it by ending our engagement.'

Again there was a silent nod from Silas, then he said musingly, 'I guessed it was something like that. He's a mighty proud man at that.'

Jenny smiled ruefully at this. 'In that, I entirely agree with you. For the record, he was wrong, you know. Not that it matters now. What I'm trying to say is that trust is an absolute must for a happy marriage, and he hadn't got that trust, not with me anyway.' She looked up from the wine glass that she had been studying on the table before her and met her host's sympathetic eyes. 'No, Mr Hawter, he didn't hurt me, not in the way you think he did. I was more hurt by the accusations he flung at me than the ending of the engagement. You might not believe that, but it's the truth,' she said simply.

This time it was Silas Hawter who let out a short sigh. 'I wish we'd had this talk two years ago,' he said slowly. 'I knew something was eating him, but he just clammed up on me. Couldn't put my finger on just what was wrong with him. He spent most of that time in the States,' he explained to her. 'More than was necessary. It was as if he was sitting something out,' he gave Jenny a wry grin, 'and he was, wasn't he?' and at Jenny's sceptical look he carried on with, 'Well, you didn't see him at that time, I did, but you can take my word for it, if it didn't go hard with you, it went hard with him, and that's for sure.'

Jenny saw no point in contradicting him on this. Mark had probably been a very frustrated man at that time, not because he loved her, but because for once he had failed to achieve his target.

A drawled 'Hi, Silas,' from the next table made Jenny remember that Mark had occupied the same table, and a horrible thought that he might have been listening to their conversation went through her mind. However, a swift glance towards the table as Silas Hawter returned the greeting reassured her on this, because Mark was deep in conversation with another guest who had evidently been there for quite some time.

'It was only,' resumed Silas a few minutes later, 'after I'd met up with a friend of his from the U.K., and was told to tell him that Peacock's Walk looked like coming on the market in the near future, that I got the connection.' He shot Jenny a quick look under his grey eyebrows. 'You've never seen such a change in a man. He'd packed within a matter of hours, and caught the next flight out to the U.K.'

He stubbed out his cigar. 'And that brings us to Dilys. It's a long time since I saw her really smile, and that's saying a lot for a girl of only twenty—although you'd never know it from the way she gets herself up these days. All in aid of catching Mark's eye, of course, and no amount of advice to look elsewhere would serve. I guess,' he added on a sad note, 'that I had some idea of trying to make things come right for her.' He gave a wry grimace as he met Jenny's eyes. 'Call me an interfering old man, if you like, and I'd understand. You see,' he ended slowly, 'Dilys has what it takes to snare a man. She's quite a little beauty, even though I say it myself, and I know Mark is fond of her. Given time, it could work out, but it looks as though he's got a few ghosts to lay first.'

CHAPTER FOUR

In view of what Silas Hawter had told her the previous evening, and which had caused her to re-examine her earlier relationship with Mark, it was an extremely wary Jenny that turned up for work the following morning.

To hear Silas Hawter tell it, she had broken Mark's heart, and no matter how hard she tried to envisage this state of affairs, it just didn't jell with what she knew of him. Men with broken hearts didn't rave and shout at their beloved, did they? or give them no chance of defending themselves from the charges flung at them. More often than not, they would close their eyes to whatever peccadilloes they might have engaged upon, simply refusing to see any fault with the chosen one. Even so, the fact remained that he had wasted no time in putting in a bid for Peacock's Walk, and on the face of things, it certainly gave Mr Hawter's summing up of the situation a certain amount of credence; no matter how improbable it seemed to Jenny.

This time she found Mark installed behind his desk, and met his cheerful greeting of, 'Good morning, Jenny,' with equable calm, and as she settled herself behind her desk she noted that there was no sign of her previous day's work, that Malcolm normally signed and placed back on her desk for her to get off to the post. Mark must have come back to the office some time later and seen to them, she presumed, although he said nothing about them. It was some comfort to know that her work had been satisfactory she thought, and wondered just how long this state of affairs would exist.

It was during their coffee break that the personal note that Jenny was dreading would eventually enter the conversation began with a casual, 'How did you enjoy your dinner date last night?' from Mark.

'Very much,' answered Jenny cautiously, not sure how much more to add to this short statement.

'Tell you about Dilys?' he asked abruptly, and gave her a mocking look that took in her slight flush.

'As a matter of fact, he did,' she replied coldly, thinking it was hardly gentlemanly of him to mention the girl. It also occurred to her that he must have had some idea of what else they had talked about, and she hastily applied herself to a list of extra requirements that Dodie had sent in to the office for clearance.

'He's got a bee in his bonnet about you and me,' he said softly, and to Jenny's way of thinking, silkily.

'He had,' she replied sharply, 'But I managed to put him right on that. The niece, though, has my sympathy,' she added acidly.

'Your slip is showing,' he remarked with a grin

that widened as she sent a hasty glance down to her
knees. 'Metaphorically speaking, that is,' he
amended with amusement. 'Seriously, though,
you'll like her. She's a nice kid, in spite of the crazy
ideas she gets sometimes.'

Did he mean her attachment to him? Jenny wondered. If so, she was in full agreement with him.

'She'll be arriving on Wednesday,' he went on
casually. 'Be nice to her, won't you? I want you two
to get on.'

Jenny stared at him. Why shouldn't she be nice to
her? he surely didn't think ... 'Of course I shall
make her welcome,' she replied curtly. But I think
it's time I made one thing clear,' she added firmly.
'I've agreed to stay on as your secretary, and want
no part of your personal involvements. You are not
using me as a blind to cover your retreat from the
altar on this occasion.'

A flash of fury in his eyes showed her she had
scored a hit where it hurt most, and for a moment
it looked as if she would be made to pay for her
audacity, but his heavy lids came down over his
eyes, masking his fury as he replied smoothly, 'So
that's what you think of me, is it? Well, I hope in
time to correct that line of thought. But just remember this. I did put a ring on your finger, and that
ought to mean something to you. It was the first
and last time for me.'

As she caught the underlying bitterness in his
voice, she looked away quickly. Anyone would think
he was the only one who had got hurt—yet it was he
that had ended the engagement. It was marvellous

how one could twist the facts to suit their own requirements, but he was talking to the wrong person if he was trying to convince her that he had really cared. 'Poor Dilys,' she murmured softly.

'Silas did open up his heart to you, didn't he?' he bit back swiftly.

Jenny coloured, but her chin was high as she replied, 'He wanted to apologise for his part in misleading me as to who would really own the hotel.' With a gratified feeling she saw that the point had gone home, as his hand lying on the desk top clenched into a fist. 'I'm glad he did,' she said quietly. 'It helped me to understand. He did it because he loved his niece, and I have no quarrel with that. What I couldn't understand was why I had to be dragged into the business in the first place.' Her eyes met his coldly. 'As I said before, whatever part you've assigned to me in this rather pathetic case, I have no intention of fulfilling. Mr Hawter is now in possession of the true facts of our past association, so that lets me out, and I'm staying out,' she asserted firmly.

Her colour deepened as she watched his narrowed eyes roam almost caressingly over her face, then rest on her white throat that her sleeveless, square necked dress left exposed, and she could almost feel the caress of his lips there as she had felt in the past, and hated him for making her remember.

'So you haven't forgotten,' he said softly. 'We haven't finished, Jenny Grange—you owe me,' he added meaningly as his hard eyes met hers.

'I owe you nothing!' snapped Jenny furiously, feeling her heart start to palpitate. She had to get a hold on herself or she was lost. He was too clever for her. She hadn't been a match for him before, and she hadn't changed one iota. It couldn't be love she felt for him, so it must be a kind of fear. Tony was right, she thought wildly, she ought to have got out while the going was good. He did intend to use her as a cover against the unfortunate Dilys, but it wouldn't stop at that, not if the look he had given her a moment ago was anything to go by.

'Don't panic,' he said smoothly, taking full note of her wide eyes that so clearly mirrored her thoughts. 'We've plenty of time. I don't intend to rush you. This time you'll come to me—you have my word on that. As for wanting you to play a part —since when,' he shot out at her, 'have I delegated such work to others? I do not,' he ended on what sounded a regretful note, appear to have left you with a favourable impression of my capabilities. However, that is something else that will soon be righted. Now, I really think it's time we got down to some work, don't you?' he asked the still bemused Jenny, who started at his swift change of conversation, and searched for her notepad with fingers that trembled slightly.

With Mark's assurance that he did not intend to push her into any situation without her full agreement, Jenny was able to relax her guard in the days that followed. That he was a man of his word she had no doubt, and in this instance she trusted him completely, and was even a little amused at his firm assumption that she would eventually break down under his compelling magnetism. Which only went to show, she told herself dryly, how much success he must have had with other women. The only thing that did worry her was that he was by no means a patient man, in spite of his calm remark about there being 'plenty of time'.

It did occur to her that it might be a good idea if she joined forces with his latest conquest, Dilys. With the two of them hanging round his neck, he might well beat a hasty retreat from the scene on the excuse of urgent business elsewhere! But Jenny couldn't trust herself to come out of such a situation entirely unscathed. Being in constant company with him, hearing his deep voice, and watching the dexterous way he handled his 'kingdom', she could well understand his fatal attraction to the opposite sex. He was so sure of himself, and, she had to admit a little grudgingly, a good boss to work for, and would find herself giving him surreptitious looks when she thought he was otherwise engaged. A chance remark of his after she had watched him on one occasion of, 'Wrong tie?' proved that he had been fully aware of her scrutiny, and had made her vow never to be caught out like that again.

That he was a good boss was borne home to her very shortly after he had taken over the hotel, for Tony's efforts to find Boots another situation came sadly unstuck after Boots had had a session with Mark shortly after handing in his notice.

'He took it back,' said Tony disgustedly, 'and no matter how hard I tried to point out that a higher salary was no guarantee for future employment, he wouldn't listen to me. Same with Flo,' he complained. 'I sounded her out on a job that was going at the Oxford, and that's a good place to get in at, but she wouldn't even consider it. Seems she's got a rise, too.' He gave Jenny a gloomy look. 'He's got them all hypnotised. I even caught Dodie giving him an approving nod the other day,' he added perplexedly, and gave Jenny a hard stare. 'I hope you're not joining the band waggon,' he said accusingly.

Jenny smiled at this. 'No hope,' she replied brightly. 'Not in the way you mean, anyway,' and what Tony didn't know wouldn't worry him, she thought sagely, although it did strike her that there was no need for her to stay on now. It had obviously occurred to Tony, too. 'Just say the word and we'll start packing,' he said cheerfully.

Jenny looked down at her hands, then out of the window of the small dining room where she sat. It adjoined the hotel kitchen, and was where members of staff usually had their meals. The table she sat at had always been reserved for her father and herself, and looked out on to the hotel's kitchen garden at the back of the premises. Her gaze lingered on an old gnarled tree from which hung a home-made swing that Jenny had used as a child many years ago. She said nothing, but some of her thoughts were conveyed to the watchful Tony. 'It was a good idea,' he said slowly, 'but I know how you feel. I'm a bit too old to pull up roots now anyway. So we stay till we're pushed, okay?' he said brightly.

As Jenny blinked quickly to dispel the tears this capitulation on his part had brought, she gave him a misty smile and nodded, not trusting herself to say anything.

'Any idea of what changes he's got in mind for modernising?' Tony asked quickly, to take her mind off the past.

Jenny shook her head slowly. 'He hasn't said anything to me if he has. I only hope he doesn't try to turn the place into a chromium-plated palace—not that I think he will,' she added musingly. 'He's got exceptionally good taste, whatever else we might say of him,' she ended dryly.

'That's as maybe,' growled Tony, refusing to endorse this fact, 'but as long as he confines his activities to the business side, I've no quarrel with him. If he steps out of line, just shout for me, and I'll give him a few home truths that he won't forget in a hurry,' he said ferociously.

Later that day Silas sought Mark out in the office, with the request that he meet his niece at London Airport the following day, as he had to attend the conference, and Jenny did not fail to note the carefully veiled annoyance that Mark felt at this request, although he agreed to meet Dilys.

It had been several days since Mark had mentioned Dilys's visit, and Jenny, with so much on her mind, had almost forgotten the girl. Now she found she was curious to meet her, but more important than that, to note Mark's attitude towards her. Silas had said that Mark was 'fond' of Dilys, and woman-like, Jenny couldn't help wondering if Mark had given the girl cause for her devotion, and if so, she felt genuinely sorry for her. She knew from experience what it felt like to be swept off her feet and then dropped when the attraction faded. If he had treated Dilys as he had treated her, then she would do all in her power to assist Silas Hawter in his quest for his niece's happiness. How, she couldn't at that moment in time exactly see, but if Mark wanted to give the impression that he was still keen on her, she would find some way of disproving this fact in a manner that left no room for doubt, and there would be nothing Mark could do about it, short of strangling her, that was!

The following morning, Jenny had time on her hands. With Mark detailed to meet Dilys at the airport, it did not take her long to clear up a few odd jobs that had been left over from the previous day, and now that she had done that, she was at a loose end, although the rest of the hotel was busy preparing for a second influx of guests. The change-over was due that day and meant a lot of feverish activity on the part of the staff.

As yet there was no sign of Silas Hawter departing, although the conference ended that day. Jenny presumed he meant to stay until things between her and Mark, or she hoped between Dilys and Mark, had worked themselves out, and if it depended on the outcome between her and Mark, then he was due for a very long visit, she thought.

After coffee break that morning she made her

way down to the hotel foyer, with the intention of giving a hand wherever help was required. She had often done this in the past when the hotel had once before been a going concern, but those days seemed very far away now. She sensed the busy almost impersonal atmosphere of the well trained staff as they passed her on their separate duties, and had an odd feeling that she was slightly de trop, and that her offer of help might well be kindly, but firmly refused, and this made her feel sad, even though she knew there was now ample staff to cope with the work, for more staff had been taken on since Mark had taken over. Even Rose, she thought sadly, had failed to notice her appearance, and was intent on studying a list of some kind, probably familiarising herself with the names of the incoming guests.

A pile of the daily papers lay on the small occasional table next to the dining room. They were normally taken through to the lounge each day, and as this had not yet been attended to, Jenny picked them up and took them through to the lounge.

She was on her way out of the lounge when the words 'Isn't it quaint?' came through from the dining room, and as the accent was American, Jenny presumed Miss Dilys Hawter had arrived.

Not wanting it to look as if she was eavesdropping, she started to leave the lounge by the side door that was used only by the staff, and heard Mark's deep well-modulated voice answer as she reached the door. 'Quaint's hardly the word,' he said dryly. 'Antiquated is the word, I think. Still, your compatriots are of the same opinion as you are, apparently.'

The girl chuckled. 'You've no sentiment, Mark,' she teased him lightly. 'Sure, they'll go for it, lifts or no lifts. Are you going to modernise it?' she queried, adding swiftly, 'I do hope not. I think it would be a pity to alter it.'

Although Jenny was halfway through the door she couldn't resist waiting to hear his answer. It was a question she had so much wanted to ask him herself, but was hardly able to do so, not in her present position.

'Lifts, probably,' he replied. 'They ought to have been put in years ago, but Peacock was not a business man, he was a sentimentalist, and it didn't pay.'

There was a harshness in his voice that hadn't been there until he mentioned Malcolm, and Jenny knew a spurt of surprise that he could still be bitter about him.

'He left the business to his secretary, didn't he, and wasn't that the girl you were engaged to?' asked his companion, in what sounded like an idle way, but Jenny gently closing the door behind her sensed the strain behind the question.

Her cheeks were flushed as she made her way back to her office. It served her right for listening to their conversation. It was said that listeners did not hear any good of themselves, and so it was with her. The way the question had been framed left Jenny in no doubt of the fact that Mark's opinion on why Malcolm had left her the business was shared by Dilys, and there was nothing she could do about it, even if she had wanted to.

By the time Mark had brought Dilys to the office to meet her, Jenny had herself well in hand, and was able to shake the small hand Dilys held out to her with a calmness that belied her inner thoughts.

In height, Jenny had the advantage of Dilys, if only by an inch or so, but her slim, slight figure, as against the younger girl's well-endowed curvaceous one, made her appear taller than she actually was. Her eyes, Jenny noted, were a light brown, as was her hair, that was worn loose, and held back by a bandeau that matched her pink two-piece suit, that clung to her figure. The colour suited her well, thought Jenny, and no doubt Dilys was well aware of this fact. As Jenny shook her hand and murmured the conventional greeting, she saw how the girl's eyes went from her to Mark, as if trying to assess his feelings towards the woman he was once engaged to, and not wanting to jeopardise her own position by making a false move.

With the intention of giving her a lead in this direction, Jenny asked Dilys if Mr Chanter had shown her her room, and if not, she suggested she should take her along straight away and give her time to freshen up before lunch, adding with a smile that she had been allotted the room next to her uncle.

Mark's frown showed that he had not liked the 'Mr Chanter' reference one little bit, and he made his point with a, 'Since when have we stood on protocol, Jenny? Dilys is almost one of the family, and

I want you to become firm friends with her, so no
more of this "Mr Chanter" or "Miss Hawter" reference, if you please.'

Jenny didn't 'please', neither did Dilys, apparently, although Jenny did not know her sufficiently
well to be really certain, but there was something about the way her small jaw hardened that
suggested annoyance. In an oblique way, Mark had
managed to stamp Dilys categorically as a friend,
and nothing more than a friend, and this must have
given her hopes a nasty jolt.

Having clearly settled that issue between the
girls, Mark made some blithe remark about having
a few things to see to before lunch, and he would
leave the girls to get acquainted.

In the tiny silence that followed his departure,
Jenny met Dilys's downcast look with one of sympathy. 'Well, shall we find your room?' she asked
gently, not really knowing what else to say, as it was
obvious Dilys had no interest in any other subject
but Mark, and she had no intention of indulging
in small talk with Jenny.

Her drawled, 'Sure,' was said without any enthusiasm at all, and Jenny wanted to tell her just
how things were between herself and Mark, and
that she had no need to look so miserable. If Silas
Hawter was of the opinion that his niece could work
the oracle and land Mark as a husband, then there
was everything to play for. He had been right about
her looks; she was very pretty, with a sort of appealing attraction that many men would find hard to
resist. It was a pity that she had settled on Mark,

thought Jenny, for she couldn't have picked a more
elusive man—elusive, that was, where the ring of
wedding bells was concerned! But something told
her that Dilys was not as helpless as she looked, and
wouldn't give up the chase until her quarry was
actually standing at the altar with another woman
by his side!

Her thoughts on this were shortly borne out by the
way Dilys made no attempt at a friendly overture
once they were alone, and treated Jenny much as
she might have treated any of the hotel staff who
had accompanied her to her room, and once there,
Jenny had no option but to leave her to it, with the
courteous wish that she enjoy her stay at Peacock's
Walk, much as she would have done to any other
guest.

So much for Mark's wish that they should become
friends, she thought ruefully as she made her way
back to the office. You could lead a horse to water,
but you couldn't make it drink—and so it would
be between Dilys and herself! She would, of course,
be perfectly polite to Jenny in Mark's presence, but
that was as far as it would go. Without lifting a
finger she knew she had been classed an enemy to
be outflanked at all costs, and considering Jenny
was on her side, it was too ridiculous for words.

That evening, to her annoyance, she found herself making up a foursome at dinner, on Mark's
slim excuse that three would be tiresome. He had
given her no choice in the matter by blithely remarking that she could fill Dilys in on the history
angle of old Brighton, adding with a smile that took

Jenny back to their courting days, 'I'm not quite so well up on that subject as you are.'

The remark, as well as the smile, brought back memories Jenny would rather push away from her. She had been an avid student of the past history of the town she had been born in, and Mark knew this. It was during a visit to the Royal Pavilion that Mark had proposed to her, and the memory brought colour to her cheeks. If Mark had noted this, he said nothing, but Jenny had an uncomfortable feeling that his thoughts were parallel to hers.

As far as Jenny was concerned the evening was 'tiresome' indeed!—what with Dilys trying to work up some enthusiasm over the historic events of the past glories of Brighton, and Jenny trying to ignore the fact that Mark never took his eyes off her all the time she was relating the history, making Dilys's concentration slightly wander from the salient points of interest Jenny was trying to provide her with.

At least Silas gave her his undivided attention, and Jenny had to be thankful for that, but when Dilys suggested a visit to the Pavilion that was enthusiastically seconded by her uncle, she was dismayed to find that she was expected to accompany them, and no amount of excuses would serve to relieve her of this, to her way of thinking, onerous task.

If she had hoped for Mark's co-operation in getting her out of such an outing, she was disappointed, for he merely sat there smiling, and weighed in on the Hawters' side. When he nodded complacently at Dilys's eager, 'You're coming of course, aren't you, Mark?' Jenny could have spat at him, she was so furious. If he had tried to embarrass her, he couldn't have found a better way of doing it—although it was hardly likely that either Silas or Dilys knew of the personal event that had taken place between her and Mark during their last visit.

How she could be expected to conduct such a tour, not only with such memories crowding in on her, but with the very man that she shared those memories with, was beyond her comprehension.

Two days later, however, Jenny had come to the undeniable conclusion that she had been right all along in her previous summing-up of Mark's reason for introducing her to the Hawters, for it was plain to see that Dilys, as Jenny had suspected, was a very determined young lady, and had her quarry been anyone else but Mark Chanter, Jenny would have advised the unfortunate recipient of her devotion to wave the white flag! As it was, she had every confidence in Mark successfully eluding the net, and was even a little intrigued as she stood, as it were, on the sidelines, and watched battle commence.

To be strictly honest, no matter how furious she was with Mark for dragging her into the fray, she was certain that he had not encouraged Dilys in any way. If she had not been Silas Hawter's niece, then he might have flirted with her, but Jenny knew instinctively that he would respect his friendship with Silas, and as such, would do nothing to endanger it.

If Jenny was at times embarrassed by the way Dilys haunted Mark, then her uncle was no less embarrassed. Jenny felt sorry for him, for he too was a bystander, but it must have been much more difficult for him. He had a high regard for Mark, and he loved his niece. No matter how much he might hope that Dilys achieved her heart's desire, he surely knew now that Mark had no intention of marrying her, and Jenny wondered whether he had tried to instil this fact into Dilys. Perhaps he had known it would have been a useless quest, and like Jenny had to wait and see the whole miserable business through to its sad culmination. If she knew Mark, it would not be long before he called a halt to the fiasco in no uncertain terms, as Jenny was sure he would have done some time ago if it had not been for Dilys's relationship to Silas Hawter.

Her thoughts on the Pavilion outing, however, took a very different turn from the slightly sympathetic attitude she had taken against the Mark versus Dilys affair. Even though she had now reasoned out that Mark was trading on their past association to help him out of a dilemma, but dilemma or not, no man with an ounce of sensitivity would have attempted to instigate such a visit to the place that held such poignant memories to both of them. On this thought she corrected herself hastily; not to both of them—only her. Not that that would have mattered one whit to him. He had said that she owed him, hadn't he? This would have been his way of exacting some kind of penance. It was also a good way of making sure that he would not be landed with the task of escorting Dilys to the places she wished to visit.

He could have found no better way of showing her that he was completely indifferent to her feelings on this, and if she were fool enough to show her chagrin at being used in this way, then it would only give him satisfaction, and do nothing for her much deflated ego. It was at this point that Jenny recalled what Silas Hawter had said about Mark having a few ghosts to lay, and it did occur to her that maybe the trip to the Pavilion was in aid of this, only she could not believe in the credibility of this. As for laying a few ghosts, in her case it would mean raising them, after she had taken such pains to bury them.

The evening before they were due to visit the Pavilion, Dilys buttonholed Jenny as she was about to retire to her room after once again spending the evening making up a foursome at dinner at Mark's insistence, and Dilys's fury, since she had still not managed to wangle a solo date with Mark.

During dinner he had been exceptionally attentive to Jenny, and not surprisingly Dilys was on the warpath. As Jenny's quarters were on the other side of the hotel premises to Dilys's room, she was a little dismayed to find that Dilys had doubled back after saying goodnight to them all, and caught up with Jenny as she was on the point of entering her rooms.

Her grim, 'I think it's time we had a talk,' left Jenny in no doubt of her purpose, and no chance of evading the issue either.

Jenny was tired, and no matter how understanding she might have tried to be, in all fairness she did not deserve this kind of treatment—not from Mark, who was plainly enjoying her discomfiture at his very obvious attentiveness during the dinners he prevailed upon her to attend, and who reverted back to the cool, slightly distant boss during working hours—or from this girl who had set her sights on an impossible dream.

'Just what do you hope to gain by playing up to Mark?' Dilys demanded furiously. 'And don't try to act the innocent with me. I know everything— why he jilted you for a start—and if you're thinking he'll take you back, then you're wasting your time. He's playing with you. Why don't you use your head and get out?'

It was a question Jenny had asked herself not so very long ago, the 'getting out' part anyway, for there were limits to what she was prepared to put up with, home or no home, and she eyed the girl with just as much fury in her eyes. It was bad enough Mark bringing up the past without this girl who wouldn't take no for an answer bringing it up.

'Might I ask just what the past has to do with you?' she asked coldly, thinking it was about time Dilys received a few home truths, and if she wasn't very careful, she might find herself on the receiving end of the lecture her uncle, or Mark, had failed to deliver.

'Everything!' spat out Dilys. 'I love Mark—have always loved him. If you hadn't the sense to know that you couldn't play fast and loose with him, that's your bad luck. It's my turn now, and I don't intend to stand aside for you or anyone—particularly for you. If it hadn't been for the way you treated him he might well have married me by now. As it is he simply refuses to take me seriously—treats me as a little girl who doesn't know what she wants—and I'm sick of it!' Her voice had risen slightly, and Jenny felt her anger evaporate. You couldn't feel angry at someone you felt sorry for, even though they were rather tiresome.

She sighed as she asked bluntly, 'Mark told you about us, did he?'

Dilys's chin went up in a defensive manner as she replied swiftly, 'No, as a matter of fact, he didn't, but I found out what happened from an old friend of mine who married a friend of his.' She stared at the carpet at her feet, before she added, a little wistfully to Jenny's way of thinking, 'He was absolutely furious when I mentioned it to him a day or so ago, but I didn't care—I wanted him to know that I knew about you, and that I wasn't just a child that things had to be kept from as if they didn't concern me—they do!' Her face started to crumple as she said this, and Jenny was afraid that she would break down and cry her heart out on the spot, and as things were she would never forgive Jenny for bringing her to this pass.

'Of course I know he's playing with me,' she said swiftly, in an effort to bring Dilys out of her misery, and it worked, for she quickly looked up at Jenny, her eyes hopeful, yet wary. 'I would have been a fool not to know it,' went on Jenny, in a matter-of-

fact voice. 'As for "getting out", as you put it, I've
given the matter a great deal of thought.' Her eyes
swept over the room they stood in. Over the comfortable three-piece suite, the tapestry foot stool that
her father had used to rest his feet on at the end of a
hectic day. The occasional tables filled with various
bits of bric-à-brac, all of personal importance—to
her, that was, not to anybody else. It was a pleasant
room, and one that held many happy memories.

'This is the only home I have ever known,' she
said simply. 'I was born here. My father was the
hotel manager,' she added quietly. 'But I expect
you know that, too. You will also know, I presume,
that the contract I signed with your uncle, in the
mistaken belief that it was he who was purchasing
Peacock's Walk, specifically stated that I was to be
retained.' She gave a shrug of her slim shoulders; if
Dilys hadn't known this before, then it was as well
that she knew now. It wouldn't make matters right
between her and Mark, but it might bring some
understanding between the two girls.

'I knew,' she went on carefully, 'that Mark was
interested in purchasing Peacock's Walk. He'd
shown an interest in it long before I came on the
scene—in the personal sense, that was'—this was
true, for Malcolm had spoken of it to Jenny before
she had met Mark. Jenny walked over to an easy
chair before continuing and nodded towards the
other one for Dilys to either remain standing or sit
down with her. Dilys chose to remain where she
was, so Jenny went on, 'As for wanting, or even
hoping Mark would take me back—I'm afraid

you've miscalculated there. I have no wish to enter into another emotional affair with him. You don't have to believe me, but it's the truth. I also think that Mark knows this very well, and is enjoying himself at my expense—or what he thinks is my expense. There were good reasons for my staying on, quite apart from the fact that this is my home—or was my home—and they had nothing to do with any wishful thinking on my part about Mark.'

She looked up at Dilys, now concentrating with fierce intensity on the carpet at her feet. 'I don't suppose you'll listen to my advice, but I feel I ought to warn you that Mark has no intention of entering into the marriage stakes, not with you, or anyone else—and certainly not me. Why don't you go back home and let him do the running? If he's really fond of you then he'll seek you out sooner or later. He's not the kind of man who likes his mind made up for him, which is what you're trying to do, isn't it? And it just won't work,' she gently remonstrated to the now indignant Dilys.

'You're a fine one to talk about what he likes or does not like,' retorted Dilys furiously. 'If you'd known him better you wouldn't have two-timed him like that, so don't go lecturing me on what I should or shouldn't do! And I'll tell you something else— I'm not going home until I've got what I want. For one thing, I don't believe you had any other reason for staying on apart from wanting to make things up with Mark. It's not as if you had to work, is it? Your last boy-friend made sure of that—but perhaps you felt it wasn't enough—and Mark's a rich

man, isn't he? Well, whatever you've got planned in
that line isn't going to work either. I'll see to that!'

Jenny ought to have been furious, but she was too
tired of the subject to work up any such feelings,
but just sat looking at the thoroughly worked up
Dilys, absently noting the way her brown velvet
gown was cut a little lower at the cleavage than was
necessary, unless one wanted to create a diversion
in a certain quarter—and that hadn't worked either,
she thought tiredly, recalling how Mark had given
the barest attention to her all evening, which was
why she was taking it out of Jenny. Her hair had
been pulled back in a ponytail style that gave her
a youthful look quite out of keeping with the
sophisticated dress she had chosen. They ought to
have exchanged dresses, she thought with an inward
sigh. Her simply styled, cotton textured dress would
have suited Dilys far better than the brown velvet
one. Although Jenny was two years older than
Dilys, at that moment in time it felt more like ten
years.

Jenny got up and walked towards the door. If
Dilys was hoping for a slanging match with her, then
she was going to be disappointed, she thought
wearily, as she opened the door and waited for
Dilys to make her departure, adding softly as the
girl took the broad hint and flounced towards the
door, 'I'm sorry, Dilys. We could have been friends,
you know. For what it's worth, I wish you all the
success in the world where Mark Chanter is concerned.'

CHAPTER FIVE

On the day of the proposed visit to the Pavilion, Jenny found herself hoping with an almost frantic fervour that Mark would find some excuse to absent himself from the tour. Relations between herself and Dilys had markedly improved since their confrontation a day or so before, and Jenny was anxious to keep this state of affairs in being. She had managed to avoid the previous evening's dinner date, on a perfectly valid excuse that even Mark could not fault, because Dodie's daughter had arrived on a month's visit from Australia. Having a lot of visits to make during the time allotted, she had wanted to show off her new son, not only to her mother but to all her old friends at Peacock's Walk, and this included Jenny.

When Dodie insisted on Jenny spending an evening with them, to meet not only her first grandchild but the father too, whom Dodie's daughter had met while on holiday in Sydney, and subsequently married, Jenny could not turn the invitation down, even if she had wanted to, and she had accepted the invitation with an eagerness that bordered on relief.

However, there was nothing in Dilys's expression the following morning when they started out on their way to the Pavilion to suggest that she had managed to get Mark on her own, and Jenny suspected that he had found some excuse for absenting himself soon after the meal was over. This was shortly borne out by Dilys's peeved remark as they parked the Bentley in the parking space allotted for visitors to the Pavilion.

'Well, at least you got all your paperwork over with last night,' she said to Mark, as if warning him that they were going to make a day of it, and no excuse of work would serve to spoil the day.

As she accepted Silas's helping hand out of the car, Jenny sighed inwardly. Her ploy of giving Dilys a free evening with Mark had not apparently worked, and she had a nasty feeling that her plan for staying close to Silas, leaving Dilys and Mark to entertain each other, would receive the same fate, and this proved to be the case.

On entering the Pavilion, however, she saw a glimmer of hope, for she had forgotten how the visitors were shepherded along lines of fixed barriers in the form of ropes to prevent anyone wandering off course. It was just possible to walk two abreast, and that was all, so there would be no possible chance of anyone pushing ahead and re-arranging matters to suit their convenience, something that Jenny suspected Mark might try if Dilys persisted in clinging on to his arm as she was now doing.

In a remarkably short time she found that

she had slightly underestimated Mark's ingenuity
where matters of self-preservation were concerned,
for having diverted Silas's attention to a remarkably fine Chinese-style wall painting, he had somehow manoeuvred to change positions with him and
now stood next to Jenny, leaving Dilys and her
uncle to bring up the rear.

By the look Dilys sent her, anyone would have
thought it was Jenny's fault, but apart from directing a glare at Mark there was nothing Jenny could
do about it. Although she had one or two attempts
at trying the same tactics on Mark by staying over-
long admiring a gilded ceiling or the beautiful
chandelier that hung from a silver dragon sitting in
the branches of a painted palm tree in the Ban-
queting Room, she could not shake Mark off, and
had to resign herself to his company in spite of
Dilys's querulous call of, 'Wait for us!' when she
found that she and her uncle were now following
an elderly couple, who seemed more intent on doing
the tour in the shortest possible time rather than
taking in the wondrous décor.

By the time they had reached the Music Room,
with its domed ceiling of gilded scallop-shells, Jenny
had ceased to worry about Dilys or Mark, but was
lost in a world of her own. The Regency period had
always captured her imagination, and as she gazed
at the beautiful wall paintings with their red, yel-
low, and gold brush strokes of Eastern origin, she
was transported back to the days of grace, when
women wore the high-waisted flimsy gowns with
plunging necklines, and quaint poke bonnets from

under which ringlets would peep. Of gentlemen dressed in the fashion of the day, as dictated by Beau Brummel, for there was a different meaning attached to the title of 'Dandy' in those days.

At the thought of dress, Jenny found herself comparing Mark's informal wear of pale blue shirt, navy blazer and navy slacks, to the tight-fitting velvet, short-waisted coat with pointed tails, and long skin-tight breeches that depicted the Dandy of those days. To her consternation she found that he would present a fine figure of a man, and her wilful thoughts ran on unheeding as the name 'Prince Charming' automatically came to mind, and she was jerked out of her reverie with a jolt. He was not her Prince Charming, or anybody's—not even poor Dilys's!

With her abrupt curtailment of any more wishful thinking in this direction, Jenny was totally unprepared for a repeat performance from Mark on precisely the same spot on which he had chosen to propose to her two years ago. In the circumstances, she might have been forgiven for thinking she had imagined the low, 'Marry me, Jenny,' but her partially shocked senses knew very well she was not dreaming it; the firm pressure of his hand on her arm assured her of this.

As the words were said for her ears alone, it was the one crum of comfort for Jenny that Dilys could not have heard them. She shook her head in a motion that clearly showed her blind unacceptance of his proposal, whereupon the pressure on her arm increased to almost unbearable tension, and she understood the silent message he was giving her. He had meant what he had said, and was not taking no for an answer.

The rest of the tour passed in a kind of daze for Jenny, as once before she had been made to come out of her reveries of the past by a few simple words that had transported her back to the twentieth century in the space of a second. But now, unlike before, the sensation was not a pleasant one and she could have cried for Mark's insensibility in reawakening the only pleasant memories she had left of their past association.

He must have been in dire straits indeed to have thrown away his independence, although Jenny had said 'yes' before, hadn't she? and was jilted for her trouble, she thought bitterly, and if he thought she would be prepared to enter into a make-believe engagement just to throw Dilys off the scent, he had better think again!

There would not, she thought grimly, be any more chances given to Mark to bully her into acting the part he had assigned her, for she was determined to get out, here and now, and found herself almost running towards the car when they left the Pavilion. The minute they got back to Peacock's Walk, she would pack. Mark was big enough to look after himself, and if he couldn't, that was just too bad. He had gone down in her estimation; no longer would she see him as a strong character, but a weak-kneed refugee from the altar. She wished Dilys joy of him. If that was the kind of man she wanted, then she was welcome to him.

On the way back to the hotel Dilys, as Jenny had expected, suggested they make a day of it, and asked Jenny to suggest some other place they might visit, preferably somewhere with gardens—or, they could have a picnic on the beach, couldn't they? It was such a lovely day, it was a pity to waste it.

Jenny had no intention of accompanying the party anywhere once they had got back to the hotel, but thought a picnic would be a nice idea—for them that was, as she had work to do and went on to give directions as to where the more secluded beaches were to be found.

Her advice, not to mention her decision to bow out of the party, pleased Dilys who shot her an approving look, and gave her uncle an appealing one. If he were to also bow out, it would give her the solo date with Mark she had been angling for since she had arrived.

That Mark made no objection to her plan for absenting herself from their company caused Jenny some puzzlement, for apart from a swift almost calculating look he shot at her as she made her excuses, he did not override her decision—yet Jenny was well aware that if it had not suited his purpose he would not have let her get away with it. Two and two were beginning to add up to five, and Jenny did not like it, but she had to be satisfied with her small success in doing exactly what she wanted to do—something she hadn't known since Mark had made a reappearance in her life.

Her anger at being subjected to what she would describe as an encore to a very bad play had evaporated by the time they had got back to Peacock's Walk, and although still determined to get out as soon as possible, Jenny lost the urge to rush up to her rooms and start packing straight away. She had told Tony they would go when they were ready, and there was no sense in making an undignified exit from the scene. First, Tony must be consulted, and given time to gather his possessions together, also to find alternative lodgings for them until they worked something out. They would probably stay with Dodie, who had ample room in her four-bedroomed terraced house a few miles away from the hotel. To leave without telling Tony would be like giving him a slap in the face, and she couldn't do it. There was also the possibility of an out-and-out row between Tony and Mark, and Jenny would rather see things through to the bitter end than cause such a happening—especially as Tony had shown that he, like her, was not averse to staying. Peacock's Walk was just as much home to him as it was to her.

Jenny sighed as the realisation came to her that she would have to see things through. Dilys could not stay in the U.K. for ever—at least, she presumed not. She did not appear to have a job, and if she had, it must be with some organisation connected with her uncle that gave her unlimited leave. Although here Jenny had to concede that she might be taking her vacation early on in the year, since it was the beginning of May, and weatherwise not really an ideal time to pick for a holiday in England's unsettled weather, although the sunlight streaming in through her office window belied this thought.

The sunlight turned her thoughts to Mark and Dilys, now presumably sitting in some sheltered spot on Devil's Dyke overlooking the valleys of the Sussex coast, and beyond that to the sea, that on such a day would be gleaming with silver glints as the sun caught the water. She couldn't help wondering if Mark remembered the time he had taken her there, as he had so obviously remembered the exact spot he had proposed to her in the Pavilion. Would he pull Dilys close to him, as he had done her? Kiss her with the same fierce intensity? A ragged sob came into her throat at the memory, memories she had forced into oblivion under the pain of the reawakening out of the fairyland Mark had taken her to.

With an effort she pulled her thoughts away from the past. As Dilys had said, it was her turn now, and it was no time to remember that she could have got Mark back by showing him the letter Malcolm had left for her. On this thought she pulled herself out of her brooding misery that bordered on self-pity, something that Jenny normally abhorred, and reminded herself sharply of why she had not even tried to exonerate herself from his charges.

The reason, she told herself firmly, still held good, she had not really believed that she could hold Mark's love, and later events had proved this theory to her eventual cost. In the silence of the empty office she could at last admit that she did love him, would always love him, but would never trust herself to reveal that love. When all was said and done, she supposed she was a coward, too afraid to venture out into the wonderland again, too afraid of getting hurt again.

Dilys, now, would have no such qualms—how could she have? She had not been hurt—at least, not as Jenny had been hurt, although unrequited love hurt, and in that Dilys had her entire sympathy. No matter how fickle Mark might be, he would not have proposed again to Jenny, and then place himself at the mercy of the determined Dilys, making no attempt to wriggle out of the proposed picnic, even though he knew full well that Silas would accede to Dilys's unspoken plea and find some excuse for not accompanying them. He would not do this without some good reason, and Jenny wondered what that reason was, although she half suspected what it might be, and if she were right, then Dilys might well be heading home sooner than planned.

Mark and Dilys returned just before five, and Jenny, who had gone down to reception to collect her evening paper, was just in time to witness Dilys's wild rush for the stairs in a way that suggested that her previous suppositions regarding the reason why Mark had allowed himself to be coerced into a solo date with her had proved correct. At the grim expression on Mark's face, she also surmised that it had not been a pleasant task. As he had not seen her as he swept into the entrance of the hotel, Jenny kept out of his vicinity by going in the other direction.

A visit by Dodie later that evening to Jenny gave her further confirmation of what had taken place between Dilys and Mark that afternoon. Dodie had always kept an eye on the comings and goings of the guests, purely in an effort to ensure the smooth running of the hotel, and to make certain the guests were provided with good service.

'Just might be a storm in a teacup, as you might say,' said Dodie, 'but according to Rose, she was in a rare taking when she came in earlier. She didn't come down to dinner, so I sent a tray up to her, but she wouldn't even open her door for Kathy to take it in. Kathy says she shouted at her to go away.' She looked at Jenny. 'Anyway, I thought I'd better tell you. Happen her uncle knows. She usually sits with him at dinner, doesn't she? and he's having dinner with Mr Chanter.'

Jenny smiled at her. 'Thanks for telling me, Dodie. I'll pop along to see her in a minute. She's probably got a headache or something. I'll take along some aspirin, in case she needs them.' She glanced at her wrist watch. 'It's time you went,' she scolded her affectionately.

'I'm just off,' replied Dodie comfortably. 'Happen she needs someone like you to talk to—you've been through it too, haven't you?' and on this shrewd observation she made her exit.

So much for her glib explanation of what was wrong with Dilys, thought Jenny wryly. You couldn't pull the wool over Dodie's eyes, she'd as good as told her that by that last comment of hers. It would be the same with the rest of the staff, she thought. They would have had to be blind not to see that Dilys was in love with Mark, or that she haunted his every movement with a determination not far short of hounding.

Although Jenny felt sorry for Dilys, she also felt exasperated. If she had only had just a little pride, she could have been saved a lot of embarrassment—not only her, but her uncle, too—and Mark, of course, for although Jenny suspected that the staff, the older ones anyway, were of the opinion that Mark had probably encouraged her. She knew this was not so, but it would be a waste of breath to actually say so.

A few minutes later Jenny was knocking on Dilys's door. She couldn't really see what good she could do, but at least she would make an effort. If it were her, she would want to be left alone, and so it was with Dilys. 'Dilys? It's Jenny. Can I come in?' she queried.

'Go away!' answered Dilys in a strangled voice that held the thickness of tears in it. 'Leave me alone! You're the last person I want around. Haven't you done enough damage?' she accused Jenny, her voice rising to a pitch of hysteria.

Jenny turned away after saying quietly, 'Very well, I'll leave you.' There was no point in staying after that, no point in arguing her case either, not behind a locked door, or against the prejudiced view Dilys held against her. Even if she opened the door to her there would still be an impregnable barrier between them.

As Jenny made her way back to her quarters, she was not indignant or even hurt by Dilys's accusation, because she could understand Dilys's reasoning. Being unable to accept the cold stark fact that Mark did not love her—and very possibly a few other bald facts, that had had to be aired—she had badly needed a scapegoat, and Jenny had been selected.

It had been so much easier to blame someone else, she thought sadly, particularly if the truth hurt as much as she surmised it had hurt Dilys. There was but one consolation; Dilys would have to leave now. Even if she hadn't much pride where Mark was concerned, her uncle had, and Jenny was sure he would be arranging for their departure at the earliest possible date, probably the next day.

CHAPTER SIX

In the early hours of the following morning, Jenny was shaken awake by a pair of very strong arms that seemed somehow familiar, and an urgent voice commanding her to snap out of the dream state.

With a feeling of unreality she obeyed the summons, and as she jerked upright in her bed her wondering eyes blinked in confusion at Mark, now searching in her wardrobe for a wrap for her to wear, and finally finding one, had bundled her out of bed and was wrapping it round her. 'Fire,' he said curtly. 'First floor.'

Jenny was now wide awake, and bent down to put her slippers on. The first floor was where most of the guests were boarded, and although there was always the risk of fire in such an establishment, she couldn't quite see how it had come about—but that could be looked into later. There were things to be done.

'Fire Brigade?' she asked quickly as her foot slipped into the slipper she had been groping for.

Mark nodded brusquely, 'All attended to,' and before she could do anything about it, she found herself picked up in his arms and carried to the door.

Surprised, she attempted to struggle out of his

grasp. 'I can walk,' she said indignantly, thinking what a fool she would look if the fire turned out to be a small blaze in someone's waste basket, and they appeared on the scene like this with all the guests looking on—not unmindful of Dilys's reaction. 'Put me down!' she repeated insistently, as Mark had shown no sign of having heard her first request and was now striding along the corridor.

Only when they reached the foyer did he pause for a moment and look down at her feathery mules. 'In those?' he asked laconically, then nodded towards the stairs that led to the first floor where guests in different stages of array were making their way down the stairs, followed by plumes of smoke issuing from somewhere above.

There was no panic, Jenny noted with approval, and she could hear Tony's voice giving instructions to a few laggardly guests to get a move on.

'All personnel are being directed to wait on the front lawn,' said Mark, as he put Jenny down. 'I want you to stay near the reception desk, and make certain they follow instructions and not hang around in here. So far, the stairs are safe to use, but I don't know how much time we've got.'

This short but concise message told Jenny the fire was a bad one, and although she knew the fire service would shortly be on hand, it was a case of urgency in getting everyone out in the shortest possible time. It was an old house, but the fire couldn't have started in a worse possible area, for the first floor consisted mainly of stout but very old oak panelling that would go up like a tinder box once the fire got a hold.

As the startled and half-asleep guests appeared on the stairway, Jenny ticked their names off on a list she had procured from Rose's records. She would have missed a few, she knew, but at least the majority were still to come.

The wail of the sirens in the distance was a welcome sound a short while later, and Jenny was able to relax a little. Her list had now been almost completed, but for Dilys and her uncle, and she presumed that Mark would have got Dilys out first, and, needless to say, her uncle too.

It was odd, though, that when she had slipped out a few minutes ago to ascertain the names of the few that had been first out of the hotel, she had not seen Dilys or her uncle, but she had not been over-worried at the time since it was possible that Silas had been helping Mark and the staff in the evacuation plan. Dilys, in all probability, was still sulking and had not chosen to show herself when Jenny had sought her whereabouts.

A second later Tony bounded down the stairs. 'Have you seen Miss Hawter?' he asked Jenny.

'No, and I didn't see her come down the stairs,' replied Jenny, now worried. 'I thought she might be outside,' and she dashed out again. This was no time to play games, she thought crossly as she approached the guests now milling around the main entrance from where she could see the staccato lights of the fire engines as they entered the driveway.

Her second enquiry proved as unsuccessful as her

first. No one had seen Miss Hawter, but someone remembered seeing Silas who had been, as Jenny suspected, giving a helping hand to Mark in keeping the blaze under control.

On re-entering the hotel, she smelt the acrid fumes that were now filling the foyer and coughed as they reached her throat. With eyes that smarted she met Tony's smoke grimed ones and shook her head. The next minute Tony was on his way back up the stairs, followed closely by Jenny. Dilys was still up there, there was no other answer.

Pausing a second to bind a handkerchief round his lower face, Tony became aware of Jenny behind him and about to overtake him. 'Not you,' he said, pulling her back. 'You do as you were told. Go and join the others on the lawn. In any case,' he muttered as he turned to continue up the stairs, 'Chanter was looking after this side, the fire started somewhere between the bathroom and the end landing. If she's still up there, he must know by now.'

A ghastly thought went through Jenny's mind just then, for she was suddenly certain that Dilys was still there. Perhaps refusing to move? Waiting perhaps for Mark to rescue her, and not budging until he came? Jenny closed her eyes—she would! She had been an extremely unhappy girl, hadn't she? Dumbly she shook her head—she wouldn't go that far, surely? If she had, it could cost her not only her life, but Mark's too.

Jenny felt sick as another unpalatable thought hit her. Dilys might even have started the fire! There had been such strict precautions taken against the risk of fire, and she just couldn't see how it had got such a hold in such a short time without some assistance.

With thoughts such as these in her mind, Jenny ignored the orders she had been given and rushed up the stairs, coughing again as the thick swirling smoke penetrated her lungs as she neared the top of the stairs.

Dilys had been given the third room on the left, she remembered, as she made her way down the corridor, now hardly able to see in front of her for the density of the smoke that got into her eyes and dimmed her sight.

With her eyes narrowed in an effort to peer through the thick screen in front of her, she saw with horror that the flames were just the other side of the room that she sought. The heat was now intense, and it seemed a matter of minutes before they would be licking at the door in front of Mark and Silas. Tony stood a little way back, but ready to give assistance when needed.

'Open the door, Dilys!' commanded Mark, whose voice was slightly muffled owing to the handkerchief he had placed, as Tony had, over the lower half of his face. Silas added his entreaty in a voice that showed that he had reached desperation point, although he made an effort to control it. 'Come on, now girl, be sensible. Unlock the door!'

'For heaven's sake, this is no time to act the fool!' Mark shouted at the still closed door.

As Jenny edged nearer to them, having some vague notion of adding her pleas to theirs, she heard the dull thuds of the actions of the firemen below, as they took charge of the situation, but even so, she doubted if they would be in time to rescue Dilys, a rescue made doubly hard by the refusal of the girl to participate.

'Answer me, Dilys. Are you all right?' Mark shouted, now sounding as desperate as Silas.

This time there was an answer, and Jenny plainly heard it. 'Go away! It's my life, and I can do what I want with it. I don't care any more!' The voice was bordering on hysteria, and Jenny felt a cold feeling play along her spine. Dilys was frightened, that much was evident, it was also evident that she would not give way, not until it was too late to do anything about it. Jenny shivered as a feeling of utter helplessness swept over her. What a stupid, wicked waste, for what? Simply because Dilys had failed to achieve her heart's desire.

Jenny's feelings were echoed by the desperate lunge the three men now made at the door, but it held firm. It was made of oak and would need a battering ram or a stout fireman's axe to break it down—if there were time for such implements to be brought into use.

As if in a dream she heard Mark's voice say very distinctly, 'Singed hair will look terrible under a wedding veil.'

Not only Jenny but the three men, it seemed, held their breath after this almost matter-of-fact statement, and although it could not have been much more than a second before the door was unlocked, it seemed a lifetime to Jenny before Dilys threw herself hysterically at Mark. 'You mean it—don't you? Say you mean it!' She waved the key in the air as she moved back towards the doorway. 'If you don't, I'm going right back in!' she warned him hysterically.

Mark's deep voice came back to Jenny as she stood in the corridor that was now being drenched with water from the firemen's hoses, but she was unheeding of the swirling water that drenched her feet, all her being was centred on Mark's inexorable answer, 'I mean it.'

The rest of that day had the same nightmarish quality about it as the early hours of the morning had had for Jenny, and for Mark, too, she noticed, as he seemed to cut himself off from all personal contact with either her or Dilys.

As far as business was concerned, he carried out his duties with the same commanding touch. Other accommodation had to be found for the guests, and having another hotel in the vicinity this was no problem for him. It was just a case of picking up a telephone and making the necessary arrangements.

When Dilys had made an appearance in the office, ostensibly seeking Mark's approval for a draft of the engagement announcement she had wanted inserted in *The Times*, she received a cold reception. 'I would prefer not to advertise the event,' he had said bluntly, leaving her in no doubt of his feelings on the matter, and Jenny had wished she could somehow become invisible, it was so embarrassing.

It was all the more embarrassing because Dilys appeared to have no idea of the enormity of her crime—and it was a crime. It was nothing short of blackmail, and it could have cost several lives, but whatever rules of propriety she had acted under they did not come under the heading of Queensberry Rules.

Love, of course, could excuse many failings, one was lucky if one went through the course of life without making some foolish action that might be excused where matters of the heart were concerned. Even so, Jenny found it hard to exonerate Dilys on those grounds, and where she might otherwise have felt sorry for her at the way Mark treated her, she was in full agreement with his handling of the situation.

Sooner or later Dilys must get the message of the lesson Mark was giving her, because it was a lesson, Jenny had no doubt of this, or that he intended to stand by his word and marry her, but the marriage would be in name only, until such time as he deemed otherwise.

Jenny could not have explained why she was so certain of this. She only knew it would be so, quite apart from the fact that Mark was not a man to be coerced into anything contrary to his nature, and forgiving did not come easy to him, as Jenny had good cause to know.

It would not take long for Dilys to realise that she might have gained a husband, but she had lost a friend. There would be no more teasing comments or smiles of indulgence such as she had received from Mark in all the years she had known him. To suddenly find herself out in the cold after being treated as Mark had himself said as, 'one of the family', would be a hurtful experience for her, and having experienced it herself, Jenny could well understand the effect it would eventually have on Dilys, who had been as coddled and watched over as Jenny had all through her life.

As far as the 'out in the cold' treatment was concerned, Jenny came in for her share too. It wasn't so much as what was said as the way he seemed to delegate all responsibility for what had happened to her account. Which was grossly unfair, she felt, since none of it would have happened if he hadn't put in a bid for Peacock's Walk—or tried to use her as a cover against Dilys's determined pursuit of a hopeless dream that would give her no happiness even though she had now attained it.

It was a kind of silent rebuke that lay heavily in the atmosphere between them in the office, and Jenny longed to shout out that it was none of her doing, and would he please stop blaming her, but as nothing was said, she was forced to hold her peace. It was a miserable situation all round. The only consolation, if it could be called a consolation, was that there was so much to do in the clearing-up process. Claims to be made out, and rebuilding on the first floor a priority, although it would not have surprised Jenny if Mark had decided against using the house as a hotel in the future, but to all intents and purposes it seemed he would, since he had given instructions for the work to be carried out at the earliest possible opportunity.

At least Jenny was saved the embarrassment of

having to probe into the cause of the fire, particularly as she suspected Dilys had somehow had a hand in it. That was up to Mark now, and she was in no position to satisfy her curiosity, even if she had wanted to. As it was, she felt the least said the soonest mended—if anything could be mended now, she thought miserably.

Mark's silent accusations had awakened her conscience over the letter Malcolm had left her, and try as she did, she couldn't dismiss a feeling of guilt that she had not shown it to Mark. That he proposed again to her had given her much cause for concern. There was just a chance that Silas Hawter had been right in that she had hurt Mark, and that he still loved her. Her breath caught in her throat when she recalled the way he had swept into her room and carried her out to safety on the night of the fire. Even though her rooms were on the ground floor, and she was not in any real danger at that time—but she had been his first thought ... Her eyes were bright with tears as she acknowledged the truth.

He loved her, and she loved him, and what a time to make such a discovery! Hard on this sombre thought came the realisation of Mark's feelings when he learnt of the contents of Malcolm's letter. She swallowed convulsively; he mustn't ever know of its existence! Of how all the bitterness and loneliness could have been avoided—of the months they had spent apart—of the tears she had shed, and her failure to understand or believe in his love for her—that part would be the most hurtful, she knew.

She also knew why she had never destroyed the

letter. She had never been able to admit to herself before that one day she would show it to him. All along she had kept that dream alive deep in the recesses of her mind, but she hadn't fooled Tony or Dodie when she had announced herself heart-free. It seemed they knew her a little better than she had known herself.

The staff's shocked reaction to the fire, those who lived out, that was, and arrived to find the remains of a charred first floor and all the resultant chaos—even if it was organised chaos—was almost numbed by another shock before the day was out. In spite of Mark's disobliging manner towards making an announcement of the engagement, Dilys refused to be discouraged, and took every opportunity of referring to Mark as 'my fiancé'—in his absence, of course, for Jenny doubted whether she would have been quite so bold in his presence, particularly after the cold reception he had afforded her that morning.

The news, as Jenny had known it would, had spread like wildfire through the hotel. There was not one member of staff who had not been aware of the fact that their new boss was a 'marked' man, for there was very little that they missed, and the way Dilys had 'haunted' him had, Jenny suspected, started a betting tote below stairs. She could even hazard a guess at the odds—of Mark evading the net so flagrantly flung in his direction, and there was no doubt that he would have gone down in their estimation at his apparent easy capture.

The only one who would derive satisfaction from this state of affairs would be Tony, she thought sadly, but in this she had wronged him, for at lunch that day he was even more morose than ever. 'That filly should have been given a firm hand years ago,' he muttered darkly. 'Easy to see she's never gone short of anything. Think she started the fire?' he asked Jenny suddenly.

Jenny looked up startled, and toyed with her dessert spoon before answering, to give herself time to think. It was more or less what she had suspected herself, but to actually say so might not be a good thing at this stage. She didn't know for certain, and if it had occurred to her and Tony, it would certainly have occurred to Mark, and it was up to him to take it from there—not that there was much he could do about it; he was not likely to press charges under the circumstances. With a light shrug she answered slowly, 'I don't know, Tony. We're lucky that the fire was contained on the first floor, and no casualties. It could have been much worse,' she reminded him in an effort to channel his thoughts elsewhere.

In this she was almost successful, but his gloomy, 'Never thought I'd feel sorry for Chanter, but he didn't stand a chance, did he?' remark just before he left her proved that his thoughts had not been diverted for long.

When he had gone, Jenny sat for a long time staring at the remains of her now cold sweet. What appetite she might have had had now deserted her, since she had only gone down to lunch to give herself a change of scene from the empty office, and stop the miserable thoughts that threatened to overwhelm her. After his first brief appearance in the office that morning, Mark had spent the rest of the time inspecting the damage, and Jenny did not expect him back that day, but knew he was around somewhere.

Quite apart from the amount of work that had to be supervised, she suspected he was keeping out of Dilys's way. The way she had breezed into the office to see him early on showed either a remarkable lack of sensitivity on her part, or a need to brazen it out, she mused. Perhaps she had wanted to determine Mark's mood, and if that were so, then she had been left in no doubt of his feelings.

A faint hope by Jenny that Dilys might gracefully bow out of the bizarre situation she had placed both Mark and herself in was quashed when Dilys sought her out later that day.

It was a meeting that Jenny had done her best to avoid, and Dilys knew it, for she must have hoped to find her in the office, but knowing Mark was unlikely to need her services that afternoon, Jenny had kept herself busy helping Dodie and the staff in the business of retrieval and cleaning up of some of the not too badly burnt furniture. In all, only three bedrooms had been affected, and only two of them needed complete redecoration. Most of the damage had been confined to the corridor which had consisted of oak panelling now beyond repair—the same with the three bedroom doors, but as Jenny had told Tony, it could have been much worse.

A tap on her door not long after she had finished work for the day announced that the peace that she had hoped to enjoy was about to be shattered, and with a nasty feeling that she knew the identity of her visitor, Jenny answered the summons.

On seeing Dilys, she groaned inwardly, and much as she would have liked to have made some excuse for not asking her in, she knew the confrontation would have to come sooner or later, and she wanted to get it over with. Dilys wanted to justify her actions, of that Jenny had no doubt, but it was her uncle she ought to be making justification to, for he had witnessed the whole embarrassing affair, and as understanding as he was, it was unlikely that he would condone his niece's conduct.

Dilys's voice, and the way her mouth had a certain stiffness about it, told Jenny of her state of mind, and her first words confirmed her feelings.

'I suppose, like Mark, you think I started the fire?' she blurted out as soon as Jenny had closed the door behind her.

Jenny's eyebrows shot up at this bald accusation, and she wondered if Mark had actually charged Dilys with it. 'Has Mark said so?' she countered quietly.

'No, he hasn't!' snapped Dilys, 'but the way he's avoiding me shows just what he thinks about it, and you've been busy making yourself scarce. I went to to the office several times today, but you were nowhere to be found.' She bit her lips hard to stop them trembling. 'Even Uncle Silas doesn't believe I had nothing to do with it,' she swallowed, 'even when I told him how it was.' Her eyes bright with unshed tears met Jenny's defiantly. 'So I'm telling you too.

I don't care what you think about what happened between Mark and me.' She gave an over-casual shrug that belied her words and showed Jenny that she did care, very much, but was doing her best to hide it.

Jenny nodded towards the settee. 'Sit down, Dilys. I'm going to, I'm tired. When I wasn't in the office, I was helping the staff to clean up some furniture— not, as you seem to think, keeping out of your way. There is an awful lot to do, you know,' she added as matter-of-factly as possible, pushing down the urge to lecture her on her shotgun tactics to secure a husband. There was also the fact that Dilys did not know that Jenny had been within earshot and had witnessed how a proposal had been wrung from Mark, and she wondered if Dilys would try to gloss over this unpalatable fact.

The calm statement somewhat soothed Dilys, and she took up Jenny's offer of a seat, and sat for a moment or two in silence while she marshalled her thoughts, her nervous fingers entwining the leather thongs of her dress belt. She was not dressed in evening wear, Jenny noticed, and that meant that she was not having dinner with Mark, or her uncle, presumably, for by now dinner would be almost over. Jenny knew arrangements had been made to provide meals for the staff, and Mark had made arrangements for Silas and Dilys to be provided with an evening meal until other arrangements had been made for them.

'I know how the fire began,' Dilys said in a low voice, her gaze now intent on the hem of her dress.

'But I didn't do anything about it.' Her eyes left the hem and met Jenny's. 'I guess, as far as that goes, I'm partially to blame. But I didn't start it.' She smoothed her dress over her knees carefully before she began again. 'Someone had thrown a cigarette end into one of those fancy canisters you keep in the corridor. I suppose there must have been some paper tissues in there that caught alight. Anyway, I saw it was smouldering when I went to the bathroom at about one o'clock.'

Her glance met Jenny's again, and there was such a look of naked misery in it that Jenny wanted to wince. 'I wasn't feeling too happy at the time,' she went on in the same low voice, 'and Peacock's Walk could burn to the ground for all I cared.' Her voice was firmer at this juncture as she relived her feelings at that time. 'I knew we were going home the next day,' she swallowed quickly, 'so it didn't matter, nothing mattered.'

Jenny listened, but did not comment on this bald statement. The thought that lives might have been lost did not apparently occur to her, but in this she had wronged Dilys.

'I never thought the fire would take such a hold,' she said simply. 'When Uncle Silas banged on my door a short while later, I was horrified, and frightened that if anyone died, it would be my fault for not reporting it, or at least trying to put the fire out. It was such a tiny flare when I saw it, I didn't dream . . .' Her voice trailed off here.

'Well, thank goodness, no one was hurt,' Jenny said consolingly, for there was no doubt that Dilys must have gone through a bad time at that stage.

Dilys nodded, and swallowed again, and Jenny knew she would tell the whole of it, and not try to cover up her subsequent actions. Jenny would have liked to have stopped her there, but she realised Dilys's need to talk about it, she would not have received a favourable hearing from either Mark or her uncle, and in the circumstances could hardly have expected one, and that left Jenny, who would rather not learn the whys and wherefores at this stage. It was enough for her to understand that Dilys had been a very frightened girl as well as an extremely unhappy one. It was small wonder, she thought with an inward sigh, that she had behaved as she had.

Dilys's gaze left Jenny and she concentrated her attention on the tip of her expensive shoes before continuing. 'I did leave the room when Uncle Silas came to get me,' she said in a low whisper. 'I got as far as the stairs,' she gulped as she looked back up at Jenny. 'There were a few people ahead of me,' she shrugged lightly, 'I suppose they'd been aroused by the other staff, and I wondered where Mark was.' She was silent for a second, then began again. 'Then I saw him—just as I got to the top of the stairs—he had you in his arms.' Her voice thickened with emotion. 'And you weren't even on the same floor— you weren't in any d-danger—yet it was you he'd g-gone to l-look after. He d-didn't care about me.'

Jenny looked away quickly from the stark misery in Dilys's eyes. There was nothing she could say to this.

'I could tell,' went on Dilys in a low vibrant

voice, 'that you hadn't liked being dragged out like
that, you were trying to make him put you down. I
suddenly couldn't bear it! He loves you—and you
couldn't care less! And I love him so much—and
he c-couldn't care less about me. I ran back to my
room.' She swallowed again. 'I had some wild idea
of making him come and get me. I wasn't going to
come out until he came.' She looked down at the
floor again after giving Jenny a quick glance that
held a mixture of dislike and yet a kind of plea to
understand how it was. 'The rest sort of happened,'
she ended simply.

Jenny said nothing for a few seconds to enable
Dilys to gain some measure of control over her feelings, then she said quietly, 'I do see how it must have
been for you, but you must understand that you
can't possibly hold Mark to that promise, the promise he gave you—was forced to give you—under such
impossible conditions,' she added gently.

Dilys's quick vehement answer shocked Jenny,
who had expected her to agree, be it miserably,
with Jenny's summing-up of the situation.

'I can—and I shall!' she said wildly, turning from
the position of a defendant defending her case to a
young vixen defending her young. 'Why should you
care! I'll make him happy. I know he's absolutely
furious with me now for pushing him into proposing
to me, but he'll get over it, you'll see. And what's
more, we'll be happy, I know we will!'

The last words ended on a desperate note, and
Jenny knew exasperatedly that she would be wasting
her breath in trying to dissuade the girl from taking

such an irrevocable step. Nevertheless, she had to try—for all their sakes. To say now that she loved Mark would only make matters worse, and make Dilys all the more determined to embark on a collision course that would only bring more unhappiness in its wake.

She tried the mild approach. 'It's very apparent that you don't know Mark very well, Dilys,' she commented, trying to keep her voice casual. 'I told you once that he was not the type of man that liked having his mind made up for him. Do you honestly believe he'll ever forgive you for blackmailing him into marriage?' At Dilys's painful flush on this bald statement, Jenny gave a slight shake of the head. 'I'm sorry, but it has to be faced, and no matter how much you try to gloss over this fact, it will always be there between you. He would have to love you very much to forgive you—and on your own admission, he doesn't—so why not be sensible about it? Pull out before it's too late. He'll respect you all the more for your honesty.'

'He does love me!' ground out Dilys. 'Only he doesn't know it. If you hadn't let him down, he wouldn't have this thing about you. He thinks it's love, but I believe he hates you for what you did to him. You say I don't know him very well, that's as much as you know. I've known him since I was twelve, and I've never stopped loving him. I cried for a week when I heard he was engaged, and I was so happy when he broke off the engagement. I knew one day he'd turn to me,' she gulped hard. 'So it didn't happen just as I'd dreamed, but it happened

—and it's going to go on happening. Sooner or later he's going to realise just what he feels about you. They say hate is akin to love, don't they? Well, he probably hates me now, and I hope he'll go on hating me—it's better than seeing me as the eternal little girl—anything's better than that!'

The slam of the door accompanied Dilys's abrupt departure, and Jenny drew in a breath of silent relief that the embarrassing interlude was over. She had tried, but as she had known it would, her attempt had failed. Dilys's attempt to make her believe that Mark hated her had also failed. It might have worked before the fire—but not now, she thought sadly.

CHAPTER SEVEN

WITH Mark only putting in brief appearances in the office, and Dilys braving it out, for there was no other way to describe her behaviour, that hovered between a kind of defiance and a bright couldn't-care-less attitude to dumb misery whenever she failed to locate Mark's whereabouts, Jenny soon found herself making plans for her departure from the scene.

There had been one or two occasions when Dilys had taken Mark's removal from her vicinity out on Jenny. She must have some idea where he had gone, etc, good secretaries always knew where their bosses were, didn't they? and so on.

It would not have been so bad for Jenny if Silas and Dilys had taken the accommodation Mark had found for them in his other hotel, but Dilys had dug her heels in and querulously demanded that some other rooms were found for them at Peacock's Walk. Only the first floor had been damaged, hadn't it? and surely they could be found some other accommodation on another floor.

It was obvious to Jenny that in spite of what Dilys had told her earlier of her determination to

see things through, she was very unsure of her ability
to actually carry it out.

What did surprise Jenny was that Dilys got her
way, and rooms were found for them on the ground
floor. Rooms that would otherwise have been alloca-
ted to staff, had the hotel been functioning normally,
and as such would not be as large or as luxurious as
the guest rooms, but this would not have worried
Dilys in the least, who saw her victory as a small ray
of hope in her wish for regaining Mark's goodwill.

Jenny, however, saw it as a small concession on
Mark's part towards Silas, who must have been
blaming himself for what had happened. He had, as
he had told Jenny, encouraged Dilys in her quest—
or at least, tried to make things come right for her,
but he could not have foreseen subsequent events.
Jenny had only met him once after the fire, and had
not missed the fact that his once ready smile had not
been forthcoming. Indeed he seemed, if anything,
apologetic towards her, and she had gone out of her
way to show him as gently as she could that she did
not hold him responsible in any way for what had
happened, as she suspected Mark had done, in his
own way.

With Dilys encamped in a room only a little way
down the corridor from her rooms, Jenny saw the
ending of her peaceful evenings, particularly if
Mark continued to absent himself from taking dinner with Dilys and Silas, and dining out elsewhere.

It was all part of the lesson he was giving Dilys,
and no amount of complaining would make the
slightest difference, Jenny knew. Mark could be

cruel, this she also knew, and it was something Dilys would have to face up to sooner or later. Try as she might, Jenny simply could not see the 'happy ever after' ending that Dilys had so defiantly predicted.

It looked as if things were at a complete impasse all the way round the bizarre affair, and if Dilys was feeling the strain, so was Jenny. She wanted to pack up and get out of what was becoming an intolerable position, with not only Mark's silent rebuke and cold attitude during the short space of time that he attended to the office affairs, but Dilys's persistent popping in on her during the evenings.

No matter which way one looked at it, Jenny was being made to feel the villain of the piece. Mark blamed her, even if he hadn't actually said so, and Dilys made no bones about it. It was the usual theme of 'if you hadn't let him down', etc, blaming Jenny for Mark's cruelty to her. Yet in spite of all this, Jenny found herself unable to break free. It was as if she were caught in a web that held her powerless, even though she knew she had only to put a few things in a case to tide her over, and she could walk out of the hotel. There would be no one to stop her, and if Dilys just happened to be in the foyer, then she would take great pleasure in waving Jenny good-bye.

Her reluctance to do this stemmed from her love for Mark, and she acknowledged this fact without reservation. As Silas Hawter had wanted to see things through, so too did Jenny. So far, no actual wedding date had been fixed, but this had not worried Dilys, who had given Jenny a detailed description of the kind of wedding dress she would wear, and the trousseau she hoped to be able to purchase.

These sort of confidences would have caused Jenny much pain if she had not realised that Dilys was indulging in a day-dream—a dream that had been there for years, always with Mark as the bridegroom.

Because she felt sorry for her, Jenny was able to stand apart and not let her confidences upset her. even while knowing that that was the sole purpose of the exercise.

Within a day, Jenny witnessed a scene that put an entirely different light on the affair, and made her start packing in earnest. If she had not chosen that moment to slip down to reception with the day's mail for Rose to post on her way home, she would not have seen Mark smile at Dilys as they passed each other in the foyer.

The smile he had given her had held the same indulgence in it that Jenny had noticed before, but it transformed Dilys, who turned on her heel and stared at Mark's retreating back as he left the hotel. There had been no conversation between them—not that it was necessary, Jenny thought miserably as she slowly retraced her steps back to the office, not wanting to risk meeting the jubilant Dilys.

As Mark had left the hotel, it did not look as if he meant to be back for dinner, and that meant another evening ruined for Jenny by Dilys's company —and Jenny didn't think she could take any more. It was bad enough listening to day-dreams when there was no possibility of them coming true, but having to listen when the improbability became a probability was something that Jenny could not do.

The only person it appeared who was day-dreaming, was herself, she thought bitterly as she searched out a suitcase and started packing. Mark had been playing with her; her first instincts had been right, and Dilys had seen it, too. She had very probably been right when she had told Jenny that Mark hated her—why else would he have made a bid for the hotel and forced his way back into her life, if it was not for revenge? As for the way he had rescued her on the night of the fire—he hadn't finished with her yet, had he? Like the cat that had cornered the mouse, it had to keep it there, adroitly cutting off all avenues of escape, until it wearied of the game.

Well, this mouse had an escape, and was taking it while the going was good. She glanced at her watch and saw that it was a few minutes past five. That meant she had three hours in which to settle her affairs. Dinner was served at seven, and Dilys usually made an appearance about eight, only this time, Jenny thought grimly, she would have to find some other confidant.

With a calmness that surprised her Jenny finished her packing, then sat down to write Mark a letter of resignation, stating that as there was so little work for her to do, she had taken the opportunity of visiting an elderly aunt of hers in Scotland. This was a blatant lie, and he would be well aware of this, as he knew Jenny had no living relatives, but it would

serve as a useful excuse to remove herself from the
scene—as far as possible, Land's End, if need be!
On the surface, it was a perfectly innocuous letter,
just right to go down on the file of personnel notices,
thus preventing any comeback from Chanter Enterprises or their illustrious boss.

The next item on her agenda was to see Tony and
put him in the picture. If he wanted to leave with
her, then there was nothing she could do about it—
Dodie either, come to that, but Jenny did not want
an en bloc decampment as she had previously wished
for, not after the fire. There was still some cleaning
up to be done, and Dodie's services would be needed
if hers and Tony's were not.

With only a few residents to provide meals for,
Tony was free to talk to Jenny when she sought him
out.

The next part was going to be the hardest part,
she knew, and past experience told her that she
would not be able to deceive Tony as to her real
reason for leaving. Now, as she sat facing him in his
personal domain in a small pantry off the kitchen,
she found she need not have worried, for Tony took
her decision with a calmness that shook her. Her
surprised eyes widened as she watched him nod
placidly when she had finished, showing that he was
in complete agreement with her.

There was no suggestion of his accompanying her
either, and this surprised her, too, but when he gave
a shamefaced grin and said, 'Dodie and I have come
to an agreement,' she understood.

'Oh, Tony! I'm so happy for you,' she said quickly. 'I don't know why you waited so long,' she added happily, completely forgetting her misery in her joy of his announcement. Tony and Dodie had been 'courting' for almost ten years. Tony had made his interest in Dodie quite plain about a year after she had become a widow, and Jenny had never been able to make out just which of the two of them was dragging their feet on the way to the altar. Perhaps Tony had not liked the way Dodie appeared to have taken to Mark, and male-like had stepped up his advances.

Back to Mark again, her heart whispered as she listened to their plans to get married in six months' time, trying to capture some of her initial pleasure in the subject, but it was too near the core of her unhappiness. First Dilys, and now Tony and Dodie.

She ought to have known that Tony wouldn't let her go without knowing where she was going, and as she hadn't as yet made any definite plans, apart from leaving Peacock's Walk, this was not easy.

'My sister runs a boarding house in Bournemouth,' Tony volunteered suggestively, seeing Jenny's perplexed frown at his enquiry as to where she would go. 'There won't be too many tourists about at this time, and the house is in the quieter section of the resort.' His eyes met Jenny's. 'You'll be well looked after there, and those sea breezes will do you the world of good.'

Jenny said nothing, but nodded dumbly. It was as good as anywhere else, and it would please Tony

and Dodie. It was also far enough away from
Brighton to ensure her a certain amount of peace,
company-wise, anyway, for she could expect very
little inner peace.

CHAPTER EIGHT

BELLE VUE, in Branksome, Dorset, was a large Victorian-looking house that stood at the end of a tree-lined avenue and was one of several residences of the same proportions. All, as far as Jenny could see from the inside of the taxi that took her to her destination, catered for the tourist trade, judging by the signboards placed by the drives that led to the houses.

Branksome was two miles from Bournemouth, and as Tony had intimated, was considered to be one of the more select areas outside the busy popular resort.

The board outside Belle Vue stated that it possessed a licensed restaurant, and was open to non-residents for evening meals, and as Jenny pressed the bell just inside the glass-panelled hallway, she tried to recall all that Tony had told her about his sister.

To her past recollection, Jenny did not think that she had ever met her, and until Tony had mentioned that she ran a boarding house, she had even forgotten that. It was not really surprising, since Tony hardly ever spoke about his private life. Peacock's

Walk had been home for him for so many years that the outside world had taken second place.

Hotel life, Jenny mused, as she saw someone approaching behind the glass door in front of her, was akin to living on board a ship. It was a world within a world, and once one became enmeshed in the life, no other occupation seemed acceptable. There was laughter, sorrow, and the inevitable drama, all enacted in front of you as if on a life-sized screen, only they didn't have to queue up to watch it, it was part and parcel of their job.

As the door opened, her questing eyes met two merry brown ones of a plump, matronly-looking woman, who was so like Tony that she couldn't be anyone else but Mrs Seaton, his sister.

'You're Jenny!' she exclaimed, as she held out a welcoming hand to her. 'You won't remember me, but I did meet you when you were about five years old!' Her twinkling eyes sobered a little as she went on, 'I haven't seen Tony for almost as long. That's the worst of both being in the same business. He keeps in touch by letter, of course, so at least I know he's all right. He rang and told me to expect you. I've strict instructions to see that you get a good rest,' she added, as she picked up Jenny's case and swept her into the house.

When Jenny unpacked a short while later, she wondered what else Tony had told his sister, for there had been a certain amount of sympathy in Mrs Seaton's eyes as she had chatted to Jenny while showing her round the house. Before leaving her, Mrs Seaton instructed her to ask for anything she required, in a way that suggested that whatever she needed would be supplied, and Jenny gratefully acknowledged the fact that Tony's sister intended to give her the best possible service during her stay.

This was underlined the following morning when she ventured down to breakfast and found that a table had been reserved for her in a small alcove in the dining room, and as it was a single table, it ensured her privacy against intrusion during her stay.

There were, of course, other guests, and as Jenny had seen on her tour, the boarding house comprised six bedrooms, two of which had been taken, and the rest, Mary Seaton had told her, were booked for the season. Many of her visitors returned year after year, and friendships started by her guests during their stay were renewed annually.

The smiling waitress who served her breakfast also brought her a small pamphlet that gave Jenny an insight into just where Branksome was on the local map, and the places worthy of a visit. Branksome Chine appeared to be the local beauty spot, and Jenny resolved to take a walk there after breakfast, and took careful note of the route shown on the map.

Her decision to visit the Chine was heartily endorsed by Mary, who popped in to see her as she was finishing her breakfast.

'Look out for the squirrels as you go through the wood,' she told Jenny. 'I know they're considered pests, but the place wouldn't be the same without them.'

It turned out that Jenny hadn't really needed to memorise the route to the Chine, as a signpost at the end of the avenue indicated the way, and all she had to do was take a slight upward track off the main road that led directly to the Chine.

As it was reasonably early in the morning, there were as yet not many people about, and she was able to savour the peace around her. The morning was a bright sunny one, and promised to be a warm day, even though summer had not yet made its appearance felt. Spring, though, had a charm of its own, Jenny thought as her eyes alighted upon the new bright green shoots of the trees awakening once again to the call of spring.

It was a time of new beginnings, and her throat constricted at the thought. A new beginning for her, too; she had got over heartbreak once, and she would again. But this time she would face it squarely, not push it to the back of her mind and pretend that she had never cared much for Mark anyway. As he had not forgiven her, so she had not forgiven him. It was the real reason why she had not shown him Malcolm's letter—no matter what else she had tried to tell herself.

At the end of the track in front of her, she could see the glint of the water as it ran down the steep cleft of the hills that overlooked the sea. The rivulets of water passed down the hillside and were flanked on either side by woods that gave the Chine a shaded, almost magical atmosphere, and for a few minutes Jenny stood entranced, watching the sunlight playing on the water, and darting in and out of the evergreens surrounding the Chine.

A sudden movement in one of the trees to her left drew her attention from the Chine, and to her delight she watched the squirrel that had broken its cover swing from tree to tree in effortless ease. Soon it was joined by other squirrels and the silent wood became alive with its furry inhabitants, all busy in their search for food.

With a sigh of partial envy at their carefree existence, Jenny continued her walk through the wood, now following a track that ran up the hillside, until she came to the top, from where she could see the sea stretched out to the horizon before her.

In a way it reminded her of Devil's Dyke, for there had been the same climb up to the view, and the same framing of trees through which one caught the first glimpse of the sea. The difference lay in the actual view at the top of the hill. Here, one could only see the sea, but at Devil's Dyke there had been the added panorama of the Sussex coast.

Not, she reminded herself hastily, that the difference detracted any of the beauty away from the scene before her eyes, and she wished miserably that she hadn't thought of Devil's Dyke, because it brought her thoughts back to Mark and Dilys.

Mark would marry Dilys, of that she was now certain. The smile he had given her proved that they had come to an understanding, and it could only be marriage. Dilys was not likely to settle for anything less, not when she was willing to withstand his fury rather than release him.

Jenny stared out to sea, hardly feeling the stiff

breeze that played on her face and ruffled her fair
hair. With misty eyes she went back to the time that
Mark had proposed again to her. What would he
have done if she had accepted his proposal? He
would have married her—of that she had no doubt
whatever. There would have been no reprieve for
either of them. The pressure of his fingers on her
arm had told her this.

She blinked to clear the mist that had formed
over her eyes. She would have then been in the same
situation as Dilys was in now. On the surface it
would have looked as though he had forgiven her,
but he would never forget what had gone before. As
far as Jenny was concerned, he wasn't the only one
who couldn't forget. Of the two of them, she was the
more to blame, because she had had the opportunity
to put things right again, and if she had married
him, the knowledge would have hung like a cloud
over her until she had told him about the letter.
There would have been slim chance of a 'happy ever
after' ending after that.

As unhappy as she was, Jenny had to admit she
had got off lightly. She might have lost her heart,
but her pride was still intact—the pride that had
taken such a hammering two years ago, when she was
made to feel a wanton by Mark's insinuations after
the reading of Malcolm's will. Her small firm chin
lifted slightly at the memory; she had since picked
up the pieces, and she would do so again, no matter
how long it took. The future was something she
simply would not think about—not then, anyway;
later perhaps when she was able to think more

clearly without the intrusion of memories she wanted to forget.

Her attempts to put a strong rein on her thoughts were undermined each morning when her eye caught a copy of *The Times* that was usually to be found on a small side table in the dining room. Invariably, as if of its own volition, her hand would reach out and pick it up from the table as she passed on the way to her table for breakfast.

After a swift glance at the headlines, she would then turn to the engagements column, dreading, yet half hopeful of finding the announcement of Mark and Dilys's engagement, and just in case it was under the 'Forthcoming Marriages' section, she studied that too.

It was a ritual she carried out each day, and when she was satisfied that as yet no announcement had been made, she was able to settle to her breakfast and plan her day with a feeling of strange relief that was at variance with her inner argument that once she saw the announcement she could relax and get on with her life again. In actual fact, however, she found herself relaxing only when no such announcement was found.

From then on, the Chine was Jenny's favourite haunt. There were enough different walks around it for her to explore, and she never tired of the views that were enhanced by the glimpses of the sparkling sea through the bright green foliage of the woods around the Chine.

She had been at Belle Vue for three days when she received a letter from Tony, and she had experienced an uneasy feeling in her stomach when she first saw the letter propped up against the condiment set on her table, only relaxing when she recognised Tony's spidery handwriting.

After enquiring after her health and hoping she was enjoying the good sea air and getting plenty of rest, he went on to give her the latest news of Peacock's Walk. The decorators were now in and making life tedious all round with their comings and goings. Mr Chanter had decided to make use of their presence and have the whole place done while they were at it. It was as well, he wrote, that she was away, as they were starting the office section the following Monday.

Dodie, he told her, sent her love, and hoped to hear from her soon. The young madam had left for the States with the declared intention of buying her trousseau—at least, Tony had added sceptically, that was what she had said, but going by a certain person's temperament these days, he suspected there had been another reason for her abrupt departure from the scene.

He concluded with the message that they were all missing her, underlining the word all, leaving Jenny with a distinct feeling that he was trying to tell her something!

When Jenny started out that morning on her usual ramble through the Chine, she was not to know that within an hour or so she would be catapulted back into the very situation she had fled from, and this time there would be no running away.

CHAPTER NINE

ALTHOUGH the morning had started off with a few clouds in the sky, by the time Jenny had walked past the Chine and up towards the cliffs overlooking the sea, the sun had peeped out giving a promise of a warm day to come, and she felt at peace with life.

Tony's letter had done much to relieve her inner tension and somehow she felt things would work out—how, she couldn't have said—but the thought that Dilys had gone back home made her suspect that she had come to her senses at last. It would be just a matter of time before the whole embarrassing incident was forgotten.

In all probability, it was Silas Hawter who had forced the issue, she mused, for Dilys was extremely fond of her uncle, and losing not only Mark's good-will but his, too, must have been more than she could take. It was obvious from Tony's letter that the understanding that Jenny had thought Mark and Dilys had come to had been very shortlived. Perhaps Mark had tried a new approach and found that it hadn't worked, so had reverted back to the polar regions of their friendship.

When she reached the top of the hill, Jenny slipped off her light coat and folded it into a soft cushion shape to sit on. The ground was slightly damp from the previous evening's dew, but would soon be dried out by the sun now shining down in warm rays, and Jenny held her head back to feel the warmth on her face.

'Shame on you, running off like that and leaving your man in the lurch!' said a voice close by.

Jenny's startled eyes met Silas's sober brown ones as she turned towards him, and with a kind of amazed dumbness she watched as he mopped his brow with a handkerchief he took from his breast pocket before settling himself down beside her.

'I'm getting too old for this kind of caper!' he said drily, as he made himself comfortable.

Her eyes were wary, even though she was forced to give him a grin. 'How on earth did you know where I was?' she queried, voicing the thought uppermost in her mind.

He smiled back at her. 'Tony—er—the chef. Didn't get round to surnames,' he told her. 'I overheard Mark badgering him for your address, so I guessed he knew where you were. Er—we had a little talk yesterday, and Hey presto! I decide to take on the role of matchmaker!'

Jenny looked away quickly. It looked as if Dilys's uncle was now indulging in day-dreams. She swallowed; who knows, she might have inherited the trait from him in the first place, she thought hysterically, concentrating on that one thought to take her mind away from what he was inferring.

'I take it you do love Mark?' he demanded, while

she was still searching for something to say to his earlier comments.

The question made her glance down at him swiftly. 'Why ... I ...' she stammered.

'This is no time to hedge,' he advised her sternly. 'But I'm willing to bet my last dollar that you do, so you'd be wasting your breath in denying it. So—he hurt you—so maybe it's pride that's holding you back, but pride's a bad master and no substitute for happiness.'

Jenny flushed and looked away again. 'Very well,' she answered in a low voice. 'But there's more to it than that,' she added wearily.

Silas patted her arm. 'Guessed there might be,' he said slowly. 'Whatever it is, surely it's not worth making three people suffer, is it?' he asked.

Her billowing hair hid her face as she shook her head silently, in bewilderment rather than agreement.

Silas sighed loudly, and Jenny had a feeling he would like to shake her, but all he said was, 'You'll have to work it out with Mark. Running away never solved anything, you know, although,' he mused, 'it finished my doubts about the way Mark felt about you. Dilys hadn't a hope.'

He was silent for a few seconds before he spoke again, then he began with, 'I guess that was my fault —what happened back there, I mean. I ought to have clamped down on her years ago. I was downright ashamed of the way she shanghaied Mark into proposing to her.' He sighed again, a much heavier sigh. 'Oh, she loves him all right. She's just not learnt she can't have everything she wants, and it's a hard lesson for her. I've never denied her anything in the past,' he shrugged his lean shoulders. 'Not that she was all that demanding, you understand, only with the sort of things kids want, but she always had the best.'

Jenny's sympathetic eyes met his as she nodded quickly. 'I did understand,' she said gently. 'I didn't approve, of course, of what she did, but she was going home the following day, wasn't she, and I suppose everything reached a climax for her. She was very unhappy.'

Silas looked at her consideringly for a second. 'You know,' he drawled, 'you're quite something. I can guess the way she plagued you after the fire. She'd have taken her misery out on you in an effort to excuse herself from her action. She used to do the same sort of thing when she was young. She knew she was in the wrong, and it was her way of saying sorry.' He shook his head again. 'She sure goes about things in a cock-eyed way, but that doesn't make her a bad girl. Even though I say it myself, she's pretty nice deep down. As for this affair with Mark, I've got to put the record straight—for her sake, as well as Mark's. She's got herself in too deep to retract, and she can be as stubborn as a mule if she wants a thing bad enough.'

As Jenny listened, her eyes followed the skyline ahead of her. Silas was only telling her what she already knew, and she couldn't understand why he had bothered to seek her out if it was only to confirm her own thinking on the matter.

'There's just one way out,' he said suddenly, making Jenny turn to look at him swiftly. 'And I've a feeling the little monkey is half hoping we'll take it.'

'We?' echoed Jenny, with a nasty feeling that he was including her in whatever the way out might be.

His answer confirmed her worst fears. '*We*,' he said firmly. 'Or rather, you,' he added, very unkindly, Jenny thought.

'Dilys says that she'll only release Mark from the engagement if you take her place,' he added calmly, so calmly, in fact, that Jenny wondered if she had heard aright.

'If——' she began, sounding almost breathless as the enormity of what he was proposing reached through to her dazed senses, and swallowed. 'Just like that!' she squeaked. 'And what exactly am I expected to do? Rush back and throw myself in his arms, in the ... in the hope that he'll have me?' she asked incredulously.

'Oh, he'll have you all right,' asserted Silas with a broad grin. 'He lacks the opportunity, that's all. He's under an obligation to marry Dilys, so he can't ask you to marry him, as Dilys knows very well. I can see what she was getting at, though. She loves him enough to let him go to the one person he wants. It's as simple as that. I also have a sneaking feeling that she's praying you'll not play ball. She's had time to weigh up the situation between you and Mark. She knows that Mark's still in love with you, and I think she's kidded herself into believing that you want nothing to do with him, and that you'll not lift a finger to do anything about it.'

Jenny experienced a wave of cold fury at the way these people were trying to organise her life. How dared they? As for Mark Chanter——! 'So Mark sent you here to tell me this, did he?' she asked in a deceptively mild voice that gave no hint of her inner fury.

'Hell, no!' he postulated indignantly, too taken back by her assumption to realise that he had indulged in the ungentlemanly habit of swearing, even if it was a mild expression of his feelings on the matter. 'That's not his way, and you should have known that. I only came by the knowledge by accident, as you might say. I overheard what Dilys said to him before I took her to the airport.' He scratched his chin in thought. 'I guess Mark was trying to make her see sense, but she wasn't having any of it. She was too wound up to notice that I was standing outside the door waiting for her.'

He gave Jenny a wry smile. 'She'll be gone about ten days. I reckon. So it's up to you, now,' he advised her hopefully. 'And don't,' he added firmly, as Jenny was about to state her feelings on the matter quite categorically, 'tell me you don't know how to go about it. You're a woman, aren't you? and the man's in love with you. Just flutter those lovely eyelashes at him, and he'll take it from there. He's not a man to let the grass grow under his feet.'

Of this Jenny was in no doubt at all, having once experienced such a relationship with Mark, but she did have doubts of whether she could successfully act the vamp, or indeed if she wanted to. Silas didn't seem to realise what he was asking of her. It was her life, and here he was, calmly stating that she should return to Peacock's Walk and present herself to Mark as if it had suddenly occurred to her that she couldn't live without him, and please would he marry her!

Her eyes widened as she tried to imagine the scene, and she closed them hurriedly as a few other possibilities entered her mind. Supposing for one moment she did just that, and Mark turned her down!—and what was worse, took great pleasure in doing so! She shook her head adamantly; 'No,' she got out vehemently. 'It's out of the question!'

Silas surveyed her sadly for a second or two. 'You disappoint me,' he said gloomily. 'I was sure mad at Dilys but at least she had the nerve to fight for the man she wanted. I guess I made a mistake about you. Okay,' he lifted his hand in a gesture of resignation, 'have it your way. So Mark will marry Dilys. He'll be trapped for life. Dilys won't have the happiness she's trying to steal for herself—and you? What about you?' he demanded. 'You'll spend the rest of your life wishing you'd had the courage to take up the challenge I've given you. If you can stand by and let that happen, then I guess Dilys was right, and you don't care one jot for Mark.'

Jenny looked down at her feet, unable to meet Silas's gaze. Then, as if the words were forced from her, she said in a low voice, 'I'll think about it.' That was all she said, not trusting herself to commit herself any further, but it seemed to satisfy Silas.

'You do just that,' he said mildly. The exasperation was gone from his voice now. To her surprise, not to mention relief, he changed the conversation by asking her if she thought there would be a spare bed at her hotel for him, for just that one night.

Jenny knew there was, but she wasn't too sure she ought to tell him this. He might have a notion of staying on a few days in an effort to persuade her to his way of thinking, and she needed time to think. Time to work up the courage he had accused her of not possessing, and goodness knows he was quite right in this. The very thought of complying with his outrageous demand gave her butterflies in her stomach, and in no way could she envisage herself taking such a role on. It just wasn't her, and she miserably wished Silas hadn't laid it on the line so baldly. That she would land up spending the rest of her life regretting her inability to take what chance fate had offered her was almost a certainty, and was too bleak to entertain right then.

That night Jenny hardly got any sleep. Silas had been successful in obtaining a room for the night, and she was sure he would expect to hear her decision before he left the next day. In any case, she could see no point in using delaying tactics. Between now and breakfast time the following morning, she would have to make up her mind one way or the other.

Coward-like, she toyed with the idea of somehow letting Mark know where she was, and leaving it all up to him. From her point of view it would be a much better way of handling things. If Silas was wrong in thinking Mark would snap up the chance of marrying her, then she had nothing to worry about—he simply would not contact her—but he had badgered Tony for her address, that much was certain.

It was while she was working out her approach to Mark, and what she would say to him, that she realised that she had made up her mind. She would do what Silas wanted her to do, and what deep in her heart she knew she had to do. When Mark had told her that she owed him, she had refused to accept the charge, but it was true, more true than he knew, because of the letter that she had kept from him.

It would be one way of easing her conscience, and even if he turned her down, she would have tried to put things right. It was not going to be easy, and she miserably wished she had as much courage as Dilys had had when it came to fighting for what she wanted; but if Dilys could sink her pride and make an all-out effort to ensnare him, she ought to be prepared to do the same.

The only saving grace lay in her feminine intuition that told her to go ahead, and Silas's dry comment of, 'You're a woman, aren't you?' In other words she had a built-in armoury with which to argue her case, particularly with a susceptible male, for the attraction was still there between them, just as strong and just as fatal as it had been before.

At breakfast the following morning an extremely tired Jenny met Silas's questing eyes with a curt nod that told him all he wanted to know. He gave her hand a squeeze as he said happily, 'Atta-girl, I knew I could depend on you.'

Nothing more was said on the subject, but it was

taken for granted that she would accompany him to Peacock's Walk that same day. If she had been asked later what she had been given for breakfast that morning, Jenny could not have said, she was too preoccupied with her thoughts to appreciate what was placed on the table in front of her, although she did make an effort and went through the motions of attempting to do the meal justice.

It was the same with the journey back to Peacock's Walk shortly after breakfast. Silas kept her entertained with stories of his youth, never once mentioning either Dilys or Mark, and for this Jenny was grateful. The miles slipped by as the car Silas had hired ate up the distance from Dorset to Sussex.

When they finally reached their destination in the late afternoon, Jenny's anxious eyes strained ahead of her as the car swept round the driveway that led to the hotel entrance. She knew her sudden return would cause some speculation among the staff, and dreaded meeting Tony or Dodie before she had thought up some plausible excuse for her return. Of course, she could just tell the truth: 'I've come to ask Mark Chanter to marry me!' and swallowed painfully at the thought—no matter how one put it, it was the plain simple truth, and beyond that one thought, her mind refused to function.

Her only hope lay in the unlikely event of no one witnessing her arrival. It might then be possible to have a word with Mark—and what a 'word' she gulped.

It was as well that Silas had placed his hand on her arm as they walked towards the entrance lobby at this point, for Jenny's courage failed her and she came to a dead stop, unable to go back or go on, and only the gentle insistent pressure of Silas's hand on her arm forced her to go forward again.

For once, fate smiled kindly on her, for the lobby was deserted as they walked through to reception, and only then did Jenny realise that her fears of meeting a member of staff were groundless, as the redecorating of the hotel meant only a skeleton staff in attendance, and no receptionist at the desk. There was only Tony and Dodie, and neither would be likely to be working anywhere near the reception area.

In her apprehensive state of mind, Jenny had forgotten that the hotel had closed down until the work to be carried out had been completed, which, she thought sardonically, just went to show what sort of a state she was in. Supposing Mark had left too, what then? The question was in her eyes as she turned to look at Silas as they walked past the desk, now covered with a dust sheet, and towards the office.

'He'll be in the office,' Silas assured her soothingly, and gave her arm a slight squeeze when they reached the office door. 'I'll be in the kitchen scrounging some liquid refreshment,' he told her as he opened the door for her, giving her no chance of changing her mind. He then gave her a slight push into the office, grinned at her, and firmly closed the door behind her.

All that Jenny had thought she might say, or had rehearsed in her silent vigil of the previous night, now deserted her as she stood uncertainly near the door, ready for flight at the slightest provocation. Her apprehensive eyes were on Mark's dark head as he bent over some paper work on his desk. For one awful minute it looked as if she would have to make her presence known, and she couldn't think how to begin the conversation—at least, not the kind of conversation Silas had thought would be so easy.

She jumped when he spoke. 'Forgotten something, have you?' Mark asked mildly, his grey eyes now studying her, yet there was something in the back of his that made her heart beat faster, and before she knew it she had answered, 'Yes, you,' in a low, but firm voice, and swallowed quickly as the full impact of her words hit her. She hadn't intended to put it so baldly—even Dilys could have done better than that!

There was an imperceptible widening of his eyes as he digested her words, then it was gone in a flash, but he kept watching her with a still, waiting expression. 'And ...?' he prompted inexorably.

Jenny swallowed again. She might just as well be hanged for a sheep as for a lamb, she told herself miserably. 'I accept your proposal,' she gabbled out before her courage deserted her, feeling as if she was stepping off a ledge into a precipice.

He could have said, 'What proposal?' she told herself, and denied that he had proposed again, or he could say that she was a little late in taking him up on it. In fact there were so many things that he could say that she gave up the speculation. She could only stand there feeling utterly lost and miserable and wishing with all her heart that he would simply get up and take her in his arms again, and tell her that he loved her.

Jenny was disappointed on all counts, since his reaction was not what she had anticipated, and her heart was heavy as she saw him quickly glance away from her and study the desk blotter in front of him. 'Silas has been talking, I gather,' he said in a voice that held a tinge of bitterness in it. 'I thought that he might have heard Dilys's farewell to me that day,' he said slowly, and glanced up at the now flushed Jenny, and startled her out of her acute embarrassment by giving a curt nod. 'So be it!' he said harshly. 'And there will be no second thoughts for either of us—understand that for a start,' he assured her as she looked at him apprehensively.

She was even more apprehensive as she watched him slowly unfold his long lean length from his chair and move towards her. There was a certain amount of purpose in his eyes that made her take a step back, although a few minutes ago she had wanted him to take her in his arms. If he had only held his arms out to her, she would have to run into them. It shouldn't be like this, she thought frantically.

'Come now,' he said in a soft almost silky voice, 'is this the way to behave with your fiancé? You've apparently forgotten quite a lot.'

The next moment Jenny felt herself pulled forward into his arms with a force that slightly winded her, and while she was recovering her breath he

gave her a kiss that melted her bones and made her
want to fling her arms about his neck as she had
once done, but some inner caution held her back.

She badly needed time to adjust herself to events,
and Mark knew it, by his drawled, 'You've got some
homework to do, haven't you?' as he kissed her
again.

This time the kiss was not only dominating but
hungry. It told of yearning, and took the form of a
punishment, as his hard lips pounded her soft ones.

The caution she had felt earlier was stronger now,
and Jenny bewilderedly accepted the punishment
he was giving her. She hadn't known quite what
to expect, but it hadn't been this. His hold was not
gentle or loverlike; it was more of a victor subjecting
his captive into total surrender. Triumphant, yet
masterful, making her want to cry out, 'Not like this,
Mark—please not like this!'

The words, however, were never uttered as she
had no opportunity to voice such a plea as his lips
gave her no respite. When his lips finally left hers,
the hold he had on her added to her discomfiture,
for she could scarcely breathe, being clamped hard
against his body.

'When I said you would come to me, this was not
the way I wanted it,' he grated out as his lips roamed
her wide forehead. 'But there's no going back now.
We marry as soon as I can arrange it.'

Precisely one week later Jenny found herself standing in front of the registrar at the Brighton register
office.

Mark had certainly lived up to his reputation of not letting the grass grow under his feet, she thought bewilderedly, as she received the tearful congratulations of Dodie who, with Tony, had acted as witnesses at the ceremony, and then having her hand shaken by an exuberant Silas, their best man.

Her feelings were very mixed at their reception, which was held at Peacock's Walk, and she was grateful that it was kept a small private affair, with only the three witnesses present.

Although it was such a small gathering, Jenny was given no chance of a private chat with either Dodie or Tony; Mark had seen to that by keeping her close to his side throughout the reception. To her amazement, however, neither of them appeared to be at all put out by this state of affairs, and took Mark's possessive attitude towards her as perfectly normal—which it would have been if things had been normal—but they were not. They had not had much notice of the wedding—as indeed, Jenny herself had not, until two days before the event, and she wondered if they were suffering from the effects of shock, since there had been no intimation that such an event would take place.

Her bemused glance rested on Tony for a brief second as she half-listened to the conversation between the men, and watched Dodie, dressed in a smart navy blue two-piece and matching beret that perched on her head, bustling round the cold buffet that had been prepared by a catering firm, in order to satisfy herself that everything was as it should be. It was then that Jenny remembered that Silas had got her address from Tony, and Tony would not have given him her address unless he was convinced he was doing the right thing. Dodie then looked up from her examination of the loaded table and met Jenny's eyes and gave her a smile that made Jenny want to rush over to her and be comforted, as she had done when she was young, particularly when she had needed assurance.

The thought made her hastily concentrate on the conversation the men were engaged in, and she looked at Mark, who was now her husband, although she found this fact hard to assimilate. His pearl-grey suit and contrasting dark grey tie fitted his tall sinewy body to perfection, and she knew a spurt of pride that this was her man. It was no wonder that she had never looked at anyone else, she thought as she saw him smile at something Silas had said, and noticed how different it made him look—so very different from the cold hard exterior he had shown her on their first meeting after the break-up of their engagement.

When his long lean fingers touched hers as he handed her a glass of champagne, she knew a thrill of anticipation as his eyes met her shy ones, then the moment was gone as he turned to say something to Tony about the date he hoped the hotel would be re-opening.

Jenny hastily sipped her champagne, and tried to look as if she was enjoying herself, but the look Mark had given her had reawakened the memory of the way he had kissed her that day, and the way he left her in no doubt that he wanted her. She swallowed quickly. Wanted her, but did not love her. Her eyes rested on the lace-edged sleeve of her dress. She had not had much time to get herself a suitable dress for her wedding, but the coffee lace dress had been the nearest thing to suit the occasion, and it had suited her fair colouring. So had the wide-brimmed chocolate brown hat, and she had been well satisfied with her appearance—yet Mark had made no mention of the fact.

As she recalled the look in his eyes a moment ago, she knew a spurt of fear. It had contained more in the nature of a threat than a promise, and was as if he had said: 'I have you now.' Dilys's words came through to her with startling clarity: 'I believe he hates you for what you did to him.' Jenny's hand that held her glass of champagne shook and she quickly put it down on the table beside her. Did he hate her—and did he hate himself for his weakness where she was concerned? What chance of happiness would there be for either of them if this was so?

CHAPTER TEN

THE time Jenny was dreading, when they would be alone together, came all too soon for her, as she stood by the door of the dining room where the reception had been held, and received a quick hug from Dodie, and firm handshakes from Silas and Tony, as they took their leave of them.

Tony and Dodie had been transferred to the Brighton hotel, Tony taking over the duties of the chef who had gone down with 'flu, and Dodie had been put in charge of training a few new members of staff, which on the face of things was an admirable arrangement, except for the fact that it left Jenny entirely on her own, and with a nasty suspicion that the arrangement had been well thought out before-hand, with just such an object in mind.

As far as she was aware no arrangements had been made for them to spend their honeymoon away from Peacock's Walk, and as Mark intended to watch over the work being carried out, it was ob-vious that they would stay there.

On her return, Jenny had taken over her old apartment, as so far that part of the hotel had not come under attention from the team of decorators working on the first floor, and gradually working their way through the whole premises. Mark had taken up his quarters in the room vacated by Dilys, and a few yards down the corridor from Jenny's rooms. At the thought of the size of Mark's room, as against her suite, it was obvious that he would move in with her, and the thought made her quake inwardly as she stood at the window of the dining room and waved farewell to their wedding guests as Silas drove them back to Brighton.

Even Silas, she thought miserably, had deserted her in her hour of need, for he had made arrangements to fly back to the States the following day, and had booked in at the Brighton hotel for the night.

She turned slowly from the window to find Mark standing watching her, and her heart turned over at the bleak expression in his eyes, and she wanted to cry out to him, 'Don't look like that. You didn't have to marry me. If only you could forget the past, we could be happy. I'll make it up to you, if you'll let me.' But no such words came, and all she could do was stand there and wait for him to make the first move. She so badly wanted a lead from him, to know what kind of future he had in store for her, and to be given a chance of adjusting herself to the swift turn of events that had catapulted her out of her uneventful existence and into a complex of strong emotions—emotions she was entirely unprepared to cope with.

'You needn't look like a martyr about to be thrown to the lions,' Mark commented dryly, although Jenny sensed a bitterness behind the words.

'I see no reason why we shouldn't carry on as we are. It's pretty obvious you need time to get used to the fact that you are now my wife. I can wait. I've got what I wanted.'

The words were bit out, and made Jenny wince inwardly. He did hate her, and pride alone kept her from breaking down and throwing herself into his arms. The fact that he wanted her would have made him make love to her, he wouldn't have been able to push her from him—and afterwards? Her breath caught in her throat. It was the aftermath that she most dreaded. For him, a physical need would be satisfied, but for her, a feeling of shame that she had given herself to a man who hated her, even though she loved him, the shame would still be there and would haunt her solitude for the rest of time.

'Thank you,' she murmured in a low voice, completely unable to look at him, terrified that he would see the desolation she felt mirrored in her eyes. He did not miss much where she was concerned, and she hoped he would put her inability to look at him down to embarrassment.

'I'm afraid I'll not be able to have dinner with you, either,' he said stiffly. 'I've a business commitment that I must keep. You'll appreciate that I haven't had much time to rearrange my affairs.'

Jenny nodded quickly, not trusting herself to answer, and after a second or so she managed to excuse herself politely from his presence, and went to her rooms.

The familiar décor acted as a tranquilliser on her shattered nerves, and she settled herself in her chair by the fireside, staring with fixed intensity around the room, savouring the solace it appeared to be offering her. She did not want this room altered, and wanted it to stay just as it was. It was her home, and haven, and she wanted no other.

Thoughts such as these took her mind off her unhappiness, but not for long. Soon she was back to her problems, and wishing with all her heart that Silas had let her be. Her marriage to Mark might have let him off Dilys's hook, but now she was snared in the net, and there was no going back, as Mark had so pointedly remarked.

It was odd, she thought satirically, that Mark was now treating her in the way that she thought he would treat Dilys should they ever marry. The dinner appointment he said he could not break—her soft lips twisted wryly; he could have put it off if he'd really wanted to. It was his wedding day, wasn't it? What other groom would be expected to keep such an appointment, no matter how long-standing?

That there was a purpose behind his action Jenny had little doubt, and she suspected that the reason was not so much to punish her as to keep a tight rein on himself. A cosy dinner for two would present quite a strain on both of them, and it was obvious that he intended to keep his distance until—she frowned as she recalled something he had said to her the day she returned to Peacock's Walk, 'This is not the way I wanted it,' or words to that effect, and that she had to go to him.

Her frown deepened. But she had gone to him. She had actually asked him to marry her—what more could she do? What was he waiting for? She knew she hadn't actually said the words 'I love you', but she would never have returned on such a quest if she had not loved him, he must surely have known that.

Whatever the answer was, it simply would not present itself, and she shook her head wearily. Until she did know, there was nothing she could do about it. Even if you hated someone, there was always one saving grace, one opinion you could both share, and as hate was akin to love, love was the stronger emotion and the key that would eventually open the door to happiness.

Jenny's eyes filled with tears, but she resolutely blinked them back. It would not do for Mark to find her crying should he decide to look in on her before he left for his dinner engagement.

In order to stem her thoughts, she got up swiftly and made her way to her bedroom to change out of her wedding dress, and selected an old favourite of hers, a sleeveless cotton dress, to wear. It might be old, but it was homely, and it didn't matter what she wore, in spite of the ring on her third finger, she told herself fiercely.

Jenny did not bother to get herself anything to eat that evening. For one thing she was not hungry, and for a second, she could not be bothered to make the journey down to the kitchen.

Shortly after ten, she decided to go to bed. She was mentally tired if not physically so, and had spent most of the evening clearing out a large old bureau in the lounge, that was full of odd knicknacks, collected during the years, and something she had so far neglected to do. Her wish that the rooms would remain as they were was a non-starter. Mark was not likely to agree to such a request. He wanted the whole premises redecorated, and as she had once heard him say, sentimentality and business did not mix.

As she settled herself in bed, she ruefully conceded that she might as well have had her cry, for Mark had not looked in on her before leaving for his dinner date, and she wondered if he was enjoying himself, and whether he had given her one thought in the whole evening.

The book she had brought to bed with her lay beside her ready for her perusal, but she did not attempt to open it. She was more tired than she had realised, and she had no need to read herself to sleep. The book was of bulky proportions, and as she tried to manoeuvre it back on the bedside cabinet it slipped from her grasp and landed with a dull thud on to the floor beside her bed, and Jenny left it there, too weary to do anything about it. She then switched off the light, and drew the bedclothes up to her chin, for the nights were still chilly in spite of the date on the calendar. Tomorrow, she told herself drowsily, she would persuade Mark to let her take up her secretarial duties again. If she had work to do she would soon settle down again—the rest was up to fate.

The following morning Jenny was up by seven-thirty, and had showered and dressed. In the early morning light it was hard for her to believe that she

was now Mrs Mark Chanter—be it in name only;
it was still an awesome thought. Another not very
welcome thought then presented itself to her. What,
for goodness' sake, was she to do with herself all day?
Mark, it appeared, still had a certain amount of
work on his hands, which of course, he would have,
he had his empire to run. At this point Jenny remembered the thought she had had before going
to sleep, that she should ask him if she could carry
on as his secretary.

He must, she thought cheerfully, need some help,
and would probably welcome her offer. It would
show him that she was in full agreement with his
decision that things should go on as normal.

The outlook already seemed much brighter to
Jenny as she started to make her bed, and as she
straightened the counterpane her elbow nudged
against a book on her bedside table and she turned
to straighten that as well. It was the same book that
she had taken to bed with her the previous night,
but she could not remember picking it up after it
had fallen by her bed. She shrugged lightly. She
must have done, otherwise how did it get back on
the table?

While she gave her hair a final brush before leaving the bedroom, she went over her movements
from the moment she awoke. She had got out of bed
and had a shower, dressed, and started to make the
bed. At no time had she picked that book up. Her
eyes widened in disbelief as the answer hit her—
Mark! It couldn't have been anyone else! He must

have called in on her when he returned from his dinner date.

No longer calm and cheerful, but flushed and indignant, Jenny visualised the scene of him standing by her bed and staring down at her while she slept. How dared he? After all that he had said about things going on as normal. If it hadn't been for the book, she wouldn't have known of his visit, she thought furiously. Her eyes narrowed in speculation. Why did he pick the book up, then? He must have known she would remember where she had left it.

Her eyes sparkled with wetness as the truth hit her. He had wanted her to know that he had looked in on her, as a jailor looks in on his charge—making sure that the prisoner was still safe in his keeping!

The fury that had possessed her quickly subsided, leaving her feeling desolated. Mark had every right to visit her in her bedroom, the ring on her third finger gave him the right, she thought bleakly. It was no use dwelling on the incident either, and certainly no use to complain; better to forget it. He was hardly likely to mention it, it was enough for him to know that she was aware of his visit.

Her slim shoulders squared as she left her rooms. As Mark appeared to want to take his duties seriously, she might as well start playing her part in their paper marriage by cooking his breakfast. Not, she told herself bleakly, that she had any idea of what his taste in the breakfast line was, but as Tony and Dodie were away, there was no one else to do it.

The smell of sizzling bacon greeted her as she entered the kitchen, and her surprised eyes stared at the woman standing by the oven attending to the cooking.

The woman was a stranger to her, and as she advanced into the kitchen Jenny saw that a tray had been prepared ready to carry into the dining room for the serving of the breakfast.

On seeing Jenny, the woman gave an uncertain smile as if not quite sure of her identity, and sounding a little flustered said, 'Mr Chanter asked for breakfast at eight,' and glanced up at the clock on the wall that gave the time as ten to eight.

Jenny felt a sinking feeling in her stomach. So Mark had arranged for someone to do the cooking for them. He might have asked her first about it; she might not have Tony's qualifications, but she could manage reasonably plain fare.

'Oh, good,' she replied, not being able to think of anything else to say. 'I just wondered if you wanted any help,' she ended lamely, but at the swift shake of the head from the woman, went on quickly with, 'I'm Jenny Gran ... er ... Chanter,' she corrected herself hastily. 'I don't believe we've met, have we?'

Mrs Cherry, as she introduced herself, appeared to be a little surprised that Jenny had not known about her. However, she soon supplied Jenny with the relevant details. It appeared she had once worked for Mark at one of his London hotels, and had since retired to Brighton, not so much on account of her age as her husband's failing health.

'Pleased as punch, I was,' she went on confidingly, 'when Mr Chanter took over the Royal last year. I knew he wouldn't forget me if he wanted extra help. I can't do full time of course, not with my Sam wanting so much doing for him, but I could help out during the staff hols, and I do. The extra cash comes in mighty handy, I can tell you.'

When Jenny was eventually able to tear herself away from the confiding Mrs Cherry, she went into the dining room and waited the arrival of Mark. Everything, it seemed, had been taken care of, and she wondered miserably whether he had fixed himself up with a secretary as well.

To her unconcealed delight, she learned a few minutes later, when Mark joined her for breakfast, that he was entirely in favour of her continuing her secretarial duties. 'I would have suggested it, if you hadn't,' he commented dryly. 'I'm getting slowly bogged down.'

With that hurdle over, Jenny was able to enjoy her breakfast—the very first with her new husband, but this thought was quickly banished as she noted the fact that although he was charming and polite to her, there were no loving looks or loverlike gestures made towards her. Just as it would have been between secretary and boss, she thought, and her throat constricted at the thought. She had wanted a lead from him, hadn't she? Well, it appeared she had got it, and it was up to her to take it from there.

It was certainly not the time to recall his visit to her last night, but she did, and she was forced to get up quickly and pick up her half finished cup of coffee, remarking as brightly as she was able, 'I think I'd better go and open the post for you—in case there's anything urgent,' she gabbled, seeing the slight lift of his autocratic brows at this rush on her part to get on with the day's work. Not giving him a chance to order her to stay put, she was out of the dining room and heading for the office as if the hounds of hell were on her trail.

When the morning's office work had been attended to, Mark suggested taking her on a tour of the hotel in order to show her the changes he had in mind, and to see whether she approved of his choice of décor. Although Jenny said nothing, the thought struck her that it was a little late in the day for any such approval, as work was well in hand, and if she had not approved, there was nothing that could be done about it.

It was, she acknowledged silently, just another way of showing her that he considered her part and parcel of his belongings, and that she belonged by his side. It was not so much that he really cared about her opinion, as Malcolm would have done, anxiously pointing out what changes he thought would be beneficial, and awaiting her approval. She sighed inwardly. Once she had taken it all for granted, not fully realising the unique position she was in—unique and honoured, she thought wretchedly, accepting Malcolm's adoration as her due, yet not realising that it was adoration—and she hadn't had the sense to see it.

By now the work on the first floor had been completed, and Jenny felt a little sad when she found

that the original oak panelling that had been destroyed by the fire had not been replaced—and it
could have been, she thought bleakly. It was not as
if Mark was short of money, he could well have
afforded to replace it, if not with oak, then with a
replica of the original wood.

Her gaze lingered on the new white panelling of
the corridor with its sculptured ceiling, and could
find no fault with it, so it was unreasonable of her
not to approve, but somehow she could find nothing
to say about it, although she sensed Mark was waiting for some comment from her. In the end she just
nodded in a generally approving way, and she knew
by the tightening of his lips that he had sensed her
true thoughts on the matter.

They then moved on and inspected the rooms.
Here again, Jenny could find no fault in his taste of
furnishings and décor, but still the sadness was
there. It was if she were being shown over one of his
other hotels, one that she had never seen before, and
her sadness grew as she realised that soon the home
she had known would no longer hold any memories
for her. It was all being slowly but surely erased.

Her heart was even heavier as she envisaged what
would be done to her rooms. After what she had seen
there was absolutely no possibility of leaving them as
they were. Not unless he wanted them to remain as
museum pieces to show what the hotel had once
looked like.

Jenny might have found things easier to take had
she not noticed Mark's quiet air of satisfaction as
their tour continued. He might be displeased with

her reaction to the changes, but it did not apparently detract from his pleasure, and the feeling gradually grew on her that there was a personal element involved.

It did not take long for her to get the answer. He wanted to erase not only the old Peacock's Walk, but all the memories that went with it! Hers, as well as his. She gulped when the realisation hit her. The fire had been a good excuse to get on with his plans, and it hadn't really made any difference, just gave him an earlier start. It wasn't only Peacock's Walk either, she mused unhappily, it was Malcolm, too, this was his way of wanting to erase Malcolm from their life for once and for all.

Remembering her earlier desperate attempts to convince him that there had been nothing between Malcolm and herself, Jenny saw little hope of succeeding now. The only hope lay in his love for her, because he did love her, a love tinged with a bitterness that impinged on hate, and somehow she had to reach through to him.

It wouldn't be today, or tomorrow, she thought sadly, but at some future date, when the bitterness had subsided, and he was able to accept her love without reservation, or recollection of what had gone before.

A short while later they were strolling in the grounds. These too were going to be altered, he told her, explaining how he had decided to have a rock fountain pool built on the lawns facing the hotel entrance.

As before Jenny listened, now with a dull acceptance of what was to be. A pool such as he was describing would certainly enhance the scene, but try as she might she could not work up any enthusiasm about it. One day, perhaps, when and if things worked out for them, she would be able to appreciate the scene.

If Jenny had thought she was now immune to any other changes, she soon found she was mistaken. They had now covered the front of the house, and were looking at the back. This was Jenny's place of childhood memories, the old swing that hung from the huge oak tree at the end of the kitchen garden, and the woods behind. Woods that she had played in sometimes with children staying at the hotel, and sometimes with Malcolm, for although that much older than her, he was not averse to playing a game of Cowboys and Indians with her for her amusement.

Until now she hadn't remembered that she had once visualised her children playing with that swing, and darting round the trees in the wood beyond, for such had been her daydreams during her courting days. She had never been clear whether she would still be actually staying there, or whether she and Mark would be visiting Malcolm, and that just went to show, she thought bitterly, how very naïve she had been.

When Mark began to unfold his future plans for this section, Jenny did not think she could take any more, and knew that when he got to the area behind the kitchen garden she would either break down or scream at him, and that would be disastrous from both their points of view.

In the event, fate intervened in the form of one of the workmen, who appeared from the rear of the house with a message for Mark. 'We'll be starting on the office walls tomorrow, guv'nor, and that safe will have to be moved. We're not sure where we ought to put it, though.'

Mark turned to Jenny, who was saying a silent thank-you for the interruption that had given her time to pull herself together. 'Anything valuable in it?' he queried. 'I confess it's a little too antiquated for my liking. I was going to have it thrown out. There's nothing of mine in there.'

Jenny narrowed her eyes in thought. She hadn't used it either. All valuables had been locked away in the desk in the office, but her father had used it, so had Malcolm. 'Only a few old files, and some personal papers of my father's,' she answered slowly. 'Nothing of much importance, though.'

Mark nodded, and spoke to the waiting man. 'Put it in the annexe next to the reception. I'll get it moved from there tomorrow.' He looked at his watch. 'About time you knocked off, isn't it?' he commented with a smile. 'Leave it for now. We'll have to get our equipment out before you start anyway.

'I think we'll call it a day, too,' he remarked to Jenny. 'Let's see if Mrs Cherry has got our tea ready.'

As Jenny walked beside him back to the house, something was niggling at the back of her mind—something important. Then she had it, and the

knowledge made her suddenly stumble in her stride
as she missed a step.

Only Mark's steadying hand on her arm saved her
from a fall, but she was too full of her discovery
to notice or thank him. The words 'nothing of importance' danced before her eyes. Oh, not important
—just Malcolm's letter, that was all! She remembered putting it with the details of Malcolm's will.
Just pushing it into the back of the safe, not really
aware of what she was doing; she hadn't been thinking too clearly at the time.

Mark must not see that letter; somehow she had to
remove it and the rest of the contents of the safe
when he was out of the office. 'I'll see to the safe
tonight,' she said hurriedly—too hurriedly, then
tried to cover up her obvious agitation with, 'It's
mostly my father's property. I don't think there's
any point in hanging on to the old ledgers, is there?'
she asked Mark, trying to sound casual about it.

'No point at all,' he replied, giving her a hard
searching look, that made Jenny look quickly away.

For the rest of that day, Jenny was in a fever of
impatience waiting for the evening, and Mark's departure for another business appointment. For once,
fate was giving her a helping hand. She didn't know
what she would have done if he had decided to can-
cel the appointment and spend the evening with
her, but he hadn't, and she had ample time to remove the letter.

That evening she went along to the dining room
for her evening meal, cooked for her by the able
Mrs Cherry, who was turning out quite a treasure,

for she did not just confine her activities to cooking, but did the odd spell of tidying up after the decorators had finished in the particular area they were working on.

By the time Jenny went to dinner, Mrs Cherry had long since departed home to her Sam, and all Jenny had to do was to try to do justice to the delicious-looking Beef Wellington.

She deliberately lingered over the meal, giving Mark plenty of time to make his departure. She had not heard him leave the previous evening, and as the dining room was at the back of the hotel, was not likely to hear him leave that night, so all she could do was to let a decent time elapse before tackling the contents of the safe.

It was nine-thirty when she considered she had given him enough time to have left for his appointment, and made her way from the dining room to the office.

With fingers that trembled a little she searched in her desk drawer for the large old key to the safe, and finding it drew in a breath of relief. She had been afraid that she might not find it, or that it had been put away somewhere in the change over of proprietors.

Even though she knew there was no likelihood of Mark returning before eleven o'clock, she wasted no time in unlocking the safe. It was as if an inner compulsion drove her on, knowing she would know no peace until she had that letter in her hands.

At last her searching fingers grasped the long white envelope; she sighed again in relief. It was safe, she had it, and now she would destroy it, as she should have done all that time ago.

'That wouldn't be Malcolm's last letter to you, would it?' asked Mark behind her, his voice sounding silky yet menacing.

Jenny stiffened and her hand closed round the envelope, crushing it in her palm as she turned to face him. Part of her saw how handsome he was; he had changed into evening dress and as usual looked immaculate, a man to be proud of. The other part of her tried to assimilate the stark fact that he knew about the letter. Her wide eyes stared back at him as she whispered, 'You knew!'

He nodded curtly and moved further into the room, and for a heartstopping second Jenny thought he was going to take the letter from her, but he went past her and stood the other side of his desk. 'He sent me a letter, too,' he said harshly, and inclined his head towards the photograph on his desk—her photograph. 'That's how I got that. It was a nice touch, don't you think?' he said bitterly.

Jenny swallowed. How much did he know? He knew about the letter, but did he know of the contents?

As if she had actually asked the questions his next words proved that he did. 'You didn't care enough to show it to me, did you?' he accused her harshly. 'Two years I waited for you to show it to me, or tell me about it. I even thought you'd destroyed it, but I had to be sure.'

Her knees felt like jelly and simply refused to support her, and she sat down in her chair by her desk. 'What can I say ...?' she got out wearily. 'How can I make you understand how it was?'

'You might have tried,' he replied savagely. 'Oh, I know what Peacock told you about me. How I played with women. How no doubt I was playing with you. I knew I was up against it, but as long as I was sure of your love, nothing else mattered.'

Jenny was bewildered. If he knew the contents of the letter then why ...? 'If you knew all along that Malcolm had lied about our association ...' she began slowly, beginning to feel a rush of fury seep through her. He had put her through all that ...

'Do you think for one minute I would have left things like that?' he demanded. 'The countless occasions I had to steel myself against acting the way I wanted to. To drag you away from this place, by the roots of your hair if necessary, but the poison had been injected, and it served as a brake against my feelings—as Peacock had known it would. Shall I tell you what he said in the letter he left me?' he said harshly. 'He told me that he'd written to you— even what it was about. He left me no illusions on that score whatsoever. He also told me that if you loved me you would show me that letter, but if you did not, then he had been right all along, that I'd stampeded you into the engagement, not giving you a chance of refusing my attentions.'

He was silent for a second or so, and when he went on there was a weariness in his voice. 'The devil of it was that he could well have been right.' His bleak gaze met Jenny's wide eyes 'I loved you enough to stampede you into marriage, too, whether you cared for me or not.' He stared down at his clenched hands. 'However, having it laid on the line like that, my hands were tied. Peacock had issued a challenge to me, and my pride had to accept it. He knew me, and he knew you, and he played on our emotions as a maestro plays a violin.'

He looked back at Jenny, now with her head bent, dumb with misery at the realisation of the unhappiness she had caused both of them. 'I believe you do love me,' he said slowly. 'I don't believe you would have come back here if you hadn't, or accepted my second proposal—a little belatedly perhaps, but nevertheless you accepted. Care to tell me why you held that letter from me?' he asked quietly, yet there was a certain amount of strain in his voice.

Jenny's eyes flew to his, and the love in hers made him take a sharp breath, but he did not move, just sat there waiting. 'Because I thought——' she began in a low voice, and gave him an appealing look. 'I'd never been in love before, Mark. I was a silly spoilt little girl. I can't explain it any other way. I didn't believe what Malcolm said about you—even though I didn't know then that he loved me too, and was trying to break the engagement. I put it down to over-protectiveness on his part, and a little bit of jealousy.' She smiled weakly. 'You did rather outshine him at school, didn't you? I remember hearing all about you, years before I actually met you. He would always hold you up as an example of the sort of person he really wanted to be, although he didn't realise it.'

She stared at her hands. 'I didn't believe what he

said, until you refused to listen to me when I tried to explain about him.' Her eyes met his briefly. 'You gave me no chance of proving my innocence. To be honest, you frightened me. I'd never met anyone like you before—I didn't know what it was like not being believed—and when you called me,' she gulped, 'his mistress, I was sure that you didn't love —couldn't love me,' she gulped. 'Not to hurt me like that. I thought you were looking for a way out of the engagement—and so did everybody else. That ... that's why ...' She couldn't go on, she was too choked.

The next minute Mark was lifting her from her chair and into his arms. 'Don't, my love,' he groaned. 'Stop punishing yourself. I played my part too, remember. How do you think I felt when I received that letter one week after the reading of the will? after what I'd accused you of? It was as well for Peacock that he'd already met his destiny,' he added savagely.

He looked down into Jenny's tear-stained eyes. 'The only good thing I can say about him was that he loved you—almost as much as I do. He couldn't have loved you more than I do, it's not possible,' he said, burying his face in her soft hair. After a moment or so, he went on, 'I believe in the end he was slightly unhinged. I think he knew that he hadn't a chance with you. Also, I suspect that he knew that you loved me, and he couldn't take it. He could have had a premonition of his death—we'll never know—but he left nothing to chance. Knowing me, he knew what my reaction would be to the

will—particularly after the lies he'd told me about
your association with him.'

He kissed the tip of her nose lightly. 'And he
knew you, my love. He gambled on the fact that
you'd be too shattered to fight back and to attempt to
clear your name.' He sighed gently. 'He was right on
both counts, wasn't he?'

Jenny said nothing but nodded her head gently.
Mark went on, 'My only hope was that time would
work the miracle. That you would miss me as much
as I missed you. I knew I only had to push myself
back into your life again and make you take me
back—but that letter stood as solid as a steel wall
between us. I'd never know if Peacock was right—
never be sure of your love. So I waited—and waited.'
His voice was low. 'The weeks passed into months,
then a year, then two years.'

He held her from him and stared searchingly into
her eyes. 'I called myself all kinds of a fool, but I
wouldn't accept the fact that you didn't love me. I
moved around a lot about that time, threw myself
into my business commitments, giving myself no
time to brood—but it didn't work. I kept tabs on
what was happening here when I was abroad. There
had been instructions left at each one of my hotels
that should any correspondence of a private nature
arrive, it should be forwarded to wherever I was at
the time. I think,' he said slowly, 'I'd got to the stage
when I would have forced the issue anyway. One
way or the other I had to know—then I heard that
you were considering putting Peacock's Walk on the

market. It was all I needed. At least it gave me a chance to see you again.'

At this point Jenny raised her eyes to his. 'You didn't act as if you wanted to see me again,' she said in a tender yet gently scolding manner. 'If I remember rightly, you were not very nice to me.'

He kissed her hard before defending himself with, 'I meant to be, but seeing you there, looking just as lovely as I remembered, made me forget all my good intentions. I wanted to sweep you into my arms and kiss the living daylights out of you. I wouldn't have left you enough breath to refuse whatever I wanted of you. So I had to do the next best thing, try and goad you into showing me that letter, if only to get your own back on me and show me what a heel I'd been in not believing you. Believe me, my love, if you had, we wouldn't be standing here now wasting precious time.' He kissed her again.

Jenny nestled against him after his lips had left hers. 'I'm so glad you decided not to go out to dinner tonight,' she murmured. 'I was going to destroy it, you know.'

'I'd worked that much out,' he growled as he held her tight. 'I knew you well enough to know that something had sparked off that panic-stricken look in your eyes, and it didn't take a master-mind to work out the connection between that and the incident of the safe.' He flicked a caressing finger under her chin. 'Never try to fool me, my love, I know your every mood. I also knew that whatever it was in that safe, it was important. It just had to be that damned letter.'

Jenny looked down at the crumpled envelope that now lay on the floor by her feet, and bent down swiftly to pick it up. Then with a slow but firm movement she drew the letter out of the envelope and handed it to Mark. 'Take it,' she said softly, 'and my heart with it.'

Later that evening, as she lay in Mark's arms on the old, comfortable settee in her sitting-room, she murmured softly, 'We've Dilys to thank for this, you know. If she hadn't forced the issue, I suppose we'd still be at loggerheads.'

'Want to bet on it?' growled Mark as his lips roamed over the nape of her neck. 'She only beat me to it by a short neck. I'd got to the end of my tether where you were concerned, and I think she knew it. I'd made plans to take you to Devil's Dyke the following day, and this time I wanted an answer from you, and it was going to be the right one, or else,' he added threateningly. 'I had to do something with Dilys breathing down my neck.' He frowned. 'I guess I was partly to blame for her actions later. I did come down hard on her, but I saw no other way. I was having enough trouble with you, without her complicating things. I didn't bother to wrap it up, I gave it her straight from the shoulder. I didn't enjoy doing it, but that was the only way to get through to her. I hadn't encouraged her, so I had no conscience about it. It was through my respect for Silas that I hadn't clamped down on her earlier. I always thought she'd grow out of it. She doesn't know it, but I think I represented the father figure complex to her. She adored her father, you know, and from things I've heard from Silas, there was a similarity between him and me. It was the reason why she would never accept her stepfather, and won't forgive her mother for marrying again.'

Jenny sighed softly. 'Poor Dilys,' she said sadly. 'We can only hope that she finds someone else, and is as happy as we are.'

'I'll second that,' Mark replied lovingly, and kissed her.

In 1976 we introduced the first 100 Harlequin Collections—a selection of titles chosen from our best sellers of the past 20 years. This series, a trip down memory lane, proved how great romantic fiction can be timeless and appealing from generation to generation. The theme of love and romance is eternal, and, when placed in the hands of talented, creative, authors whose true gift lies in their ability to write from the heart, the stories reach a special level of brilliance that the passage of time cannot dim. Like a treasured heirloom, an antique of superb craftsmanship, a beautiful gift from someone loved—these stories too, have a special significance that transcends the ordinary. **$1.25 each novel**

Here are your 1978
Harlequin Collection Editions...

Original Harlequin Romance numbers in brackets

ORDER FORM
Harlequin Reader Service

In U.S.A.
MPO Box 707
Niagara Falls, N.Y. 14302

In Canada
649 Ontario St.,
Stratford, Ontario, N5A 6W2

Please send me the following Harlequin Collection novels. I am enclosing my check or money order for $1.25 for each novel ordered, plus 25¢ to cover postage and handling.

☐ 102	☐ 115	☐ 128	☐ 140
☐ 103	☐ 116	☐ 129	☐ 141
☐ 104	☐ 117	☐ 130	☐ 142
☐ 105	☐ 118	☐ 131	☐ 143
☐ 106	☐ 119	☐ 132	☐ 144
☐ 107	☐ 120	☐ 133	☐ 145
☐ 108	☐ 121	☐ 134	☐ 146
☐ 109	☐ 122	☐ 135	☐ 147
☐ 110	☐ 123	☐ 136	☐ 148
☐ 111	☐ 124	☐ 137	☐ 149
☐ 112	☐ 125	☐ 138	☐ 150
☐ 113	☐ 126	☐ 139	☐ 151
☐ 114	☐ 127		

Number of novels checked @
$1.25 each = $ _____
N.Y. and N.J. residents add
appropriate sales tax $ _____

Postage and handling $ ___.25___

                                    TOTAL $ _____

NAME _____
                    (Please Print)
ADDRESS _____

CITY _____

STATE/PROV. _____

ZIP/POSTAL CODE _____

ABC ROM 2209

Offer expires December 31, 1978

And there's still *more* love in

Harlequin Presents...

Do you have a favorite
Harlequin author?
Then here is an
opportunity you must
not miss!

HARLEQUIN OMNIBUS

Each volume contains
3 full-length compelling
romances by one author.
Almost 600 pages of
the very best in romantic
fiction for only $2.75

A wonderful way to collect
the novels by the Harlequin
writers you love best!